One Last Notch

Buck Halliday was a fast gun – or had been in his hell-raising days – but he didn't brag about it. He left that to kill-crazy punks like Petrie and Cole.

Halliday thought those wild days were behind him until he found himself facing Abilene, the gunslinger claiming to be the fastest of them all. Buck had never dodged a showdown and it was too late to start now.

Together they went for their Colts. Now, the fate of the outlaw territory hinged on which man would walk away and which man would die.

One Last Notch

Ryan Bodie

ISBN 0 7090 7788 2

Robert Hale Limited
Clerkenwell House
Clerkenwell Green
London EC1R 0HT

Typeset by
Derek Doyle & Associates, Shaw Heath.
Printed and bound in Great Britain by
Antony Rowe Limited, Wiltshire.

CHAPTER 1

THE HARD BREED

Halliday checked his dun on the approaches to the bridge and stared at the back of the runty towner who'd started across just ahead of him.

'Howdy!' he yelled. His voice was strong, just like the rest of him.

The man quickened his pace. He was around five-two in a badly fitted green suit with baggy elbows, a ridiculous derby hat. He was probably scared, mused Halliday, who sometimes had that effect on people, especially at times like this when he'd recently been in the 'news'.

'Hey, shorty!' he yelled. 'I'm talking to you.'

The towner slowed, then stopped, and finally turned with obvious reluctance. He knew the big rider by sight and name. Halliday the part-time horse rancher, wagonmaster and occasional visitor to Paradise, Arkansas, didn't much bother him. But Halliday, the man who'd recently put both himself and

Paradise on the map when he'd cut down a trio of bandits attacking a thirty-wagon train he was bossing, certainly did.

'Sir?' the man quavered, causing the horseman to shake his big head in disgust. How could any man be this nervous and live? he mused. Particularly when there was no need. Today, Halliday considered himself just an everyday kind of man on an ordinary mission. Namely to get away from dull routine and really tie one on, the way any red-blooded Arkansas son had a right to do at the end of a straight month of solid slog, a busted romance, and only a weird Mexican vaquero for company.

He forced a grin; he wasn't an easy-smiling man.

'Just want to know if they've all gone,' he said.

'W-who, Mr Halliday sir?'

'The goddamn—' he broke off, realizing he was being testy again. His grin was phony, but it was still a grin. 'I mean the reporters and suchlike. You know, the ones from Little Rock and all over.'

'Er, all disappeared, Mr Halliday. I guess when they realized you wasn't coming back to town while they was lazing about waiting to get your side of the story, why, they just up and disappeared.'

'Fine. OK, you can get lost now – er, I mean, thanks a million, pard.'

The townsman scooted. Halliday used his knees to get the horse started and rode on to enter the main stem hard by the post office and the River Bell saloon. He ignored the stares as he swung down and tied up. Following the drama on his last drive west he knew it would take some time for folks to settle down and realize he was still the same 'easygoing' *hombre* he'd been before the shootout at Phoenix Crossing. Somewhat unsociable and tetchy at times perhaps, but definitely not the two-gun shootist the yellow press had labelled him.

He mounted the post office steps and went in. Six letters. Five from various newspapers seeking interviews, one with a heart and kisses sketched on the flap that smelled of perfume.

He sniffed the envelope and was starting to smile when the postal agent leaned on the counter and said, 'You seen them two geezers yet, Mr Halliday?'

'Huh?' He was miles away. The letter was from an old and attractive friend in the north, and couldn't be more welcome right now, considering the fact that as far as he could tell he'd just been – what was the word? Dumped, that was it. He blinked, then scowled at the clerk. 'Not more news hounds?'

The fellow shook his head. 'Uh huh. Young fellers, they are. Kinda look like college kids only they're packing iron and both got eyes like Clint Foley's pet wolf – know what I mean?'

'Gunmen?' Halliday was peeved. For a man with a turbulent past and an aggressive reputation that he was trying to live down, he figured he'd managed to put the old days and the wild ways behind him here over the past year, if you overlooked the wagon train shootout. He wanted to keep things that way and certainly didn't fancy gunmen showing up and asking after him.

'Say what they wanted, Ike?'

'Jest wanted to see you.'

'Give names?'

'Uh huh. Petrie and Cole. Ring any bells?'

He was shaking his head when he heard the door-bell chime. He turned sharply and knew who it was right off from the postman's description.

Young and lean, one dark and the other fair, yet with a curious similarity to each other that had nothing to do with physical features and everything to do with type. He felt his neck hair lift as he swung to face them squarely.

'You punks looking for me?'

That was the Halliday style. Go in hard and let them know who they were dealing with right from the jump.

'Mr Halliday?' said the dark one, showing no sign of nervousness. 'I'm Petrie, and my partner's Cole—'

'And?' he chopped in.

'And – Mr Halliday?' Cole asked. His face said twenties but the eyes were old. 'And what?'

'And what the hell do you want – and it had better be good.'

Petrie removed his flatbrim and turned it with slender fingers.

'I think you are interpreting this the wrong way, Mr Halliday,' he said in his clipped flat voice. 'We're not troublemakers or anything like. We've merely come to Paradise to deliver a personal message from an old friend of yours.'

Halliday's scowl bit deep. He still wasn't convinced.

'What friend?'

'Why, an old friend from the war who finally heard

about you after all those years when the wagon train affair made the news,' Cole supplied with the faintest suggestion of a smile. 'I'm speaking of former Colonel Ketchell Dabney of the 25th Minnesotan Cavalry.'

Halliday's jaw sagged and the blood drained slowly from his face. Stunned, his mind went clicking back over the years to the war, to burning Atlanta and a night of blood and terror he would never forget. . . .

Halliday was down again. This was the third time he'd been smashed off his feet in this grim battle to the death and it was by far the most telling knock-down yet in a wildly uneven contest. His head rang and his left arm hung useless at his side as a result of the dagger thrust that had put him down for the third time. There was blood in his mouth and a red film before his eyes that was in no way related to the wall of flames consuming stricken Atlanta, but stemmed from the weakness in him that threatened to undermine his iron will, which he was summoning to force himself to his feet just one more time.

While all about him were the snarling, stubbled faces of the gray-garbed enemy, lashing at him with clubs and sabres, taking savage pleasure in killing by inches so dangerous an enemy who'd been responsible for the deaths of several of their number before they shot his mount from under him in this smoke-filled back street of the doomed city.

Halliday was up, but swaying. He spat blood. Earlier that awful day he'd taken part in a scything cavalry charge that had been as dramatic as anything he'd experienced in the war. That morning he'd felt like a hero, a victor and immortal, but now the hounds were tearing him to pieces and all he could do was snarl and lunge impotently as they closed in for the kill.

The big one with the spade beard took him from behind, clamping a headlock around his throat and slamming him hard up against the brick wall of the East Atlanta Shipping Company.

Halliday's vision was going as the iron bar of that forearm closed off his windpipe. But somehow he managed to piston his right elbow back, driving it into a flabby gut with the force of an engine piston, drawing a gasp of pure agony from a bearded mouth. Air rushed into his lungs as that fierce grip was broken. He pivoted and dropped his big head, snapping his brow down hard full into the attacker's face.

The man fell like a stone with blood gushing from the three inch vertical split running from hairline to nose.

For a moment Halliday tasted triumph. For a handful of seconds, as the enemy held off and the adrenalin rushed through his body, he thought that by some miracle he might yet pull off the impossible. Batter his way through, run like hell, rejoin the regiment. He could do it!

But now they came at him like wolves, snarling and no longer taunting, driving in on him, striking, hurting, beating him to the ground again with their empty weapons.

Boot-heels smashed down upon him and Halliday felt himself sinking, going under with a great roaring in his ears and the bitter certitude now that the greatest civil war in history was all over for Buck Halliday, cavalryman and army scout.

'Finish the bastard, Jeb!'

The voice seemed to come from the far distance, but the soldier swinging the rifle with the bayonet attached, who loomed above him like a towering demon out of hell, was all too close.

The glittering bayonet started downwards and Halliday could only watch it descend.

It kept coming but missed. Not by mere inches but by incomprehensible feet, the dagger point snapping off as it struck the wall – hot blood splattering down over Halliday's upturned face. Enemy blood.

The dead bayonetter crashed on his face at Halliday's side as other sounds reached him, muffled, crunching sounds like distant river ice breaking up, but which he dimly recognized as rifle reports, slamming to and fro between the high walls of this smoke-shrouded back street.

His attackers were staggering away from him and Halliday dimly glimpsed movement farther along the street.

It was a tall figure attired in a uniform of the same faded blue as his own. An officer's uniform. The officer held a belching repeater rifle at waist height with his right hand while his left worked a hand gun which snarled and barked like a big angry dog, probably the loveliest sound Halliday had ever heard.

He didn't pause to ask questions. He'd never believed in miracles before but was solid ready to accept this as such at face value.

Somehow he hauled his bleeding, aching six-feet-three frame off the blood-soaked earth. The rifle and revolver continued to storm and bloodied, howling figures were tumbling and convulsing all about him. Now he was cutting a bearded corporal's stubby legs from under him with a scything, two-footed kick. He grabbed a fallen billy club and applied it vengefully to the first head within reach as he came fully erect.

He managed to inflict considerable damage while his two-gun Samaritan continued to slaughter them like Thanksgiving turkeys, killing in fact with such ruthless efficiency that finally, leaking blood and panting like a grampus, Halliday simply staggered clear, leaned his back against the wall and watched.

He began counting the shots. Four . . . five. Then it was all over. The enemy lay like crumpled heaps of dirty clothing all about him, the cobblestones running bright red. The runty corporal had taken a slug through the forehead which had erupted through the back of his head, now a broken watermelon. The officer in charge lay crumpled in a ball, shrunken in death, sightless eyes focused upwards on Halliday's face. Until that day, Halliday figured he'd witnessed enough violent death to last him a lifetime, but death had never looked so welcome as in that moment, and he was not too damned delicate to admit it.

He stared as the long-striding man in ragged colonel's uniform came towards him. Smoke and dust grimed, he slowly lowered his smoking sidearm and kicked a corpse to make sure it was dead. Then piercing blue eyes met Halliday's and he grinned broadly.

'You're a lucky man, soldier.'

'Lucky you happened along, sir.'

'Hell, I didn't just happen along.' The man turned and gestured. 'I've been watching you get the crap kicked out of you for ten minutes. It was only when I realized the scum were all out of ammunition that I decided to claim a few scalps.'

'I still owe you my life.' The words came hard despite Halliday's gratitude. 'Thanks' was one of the toughest words to get his tongue around for this cavalryman.

'Yes, you do, don't you, Lieutenant, ahh. . . ?'

'Halliday, sir. 25th Cavalry.'

'Dabney. That's Colonel Dabney to you . . .'

The officer broke off sharply as there came the sudden pounding of approaching hoofs, the rumble of wheels. Could have been Union, could just as easily be more Johnny Rebs. . . . Before Halliday could react, the officer spun away without a word and vanished between two buildings, leaving him alone.

Halliday was ready to follow. But this proved unnecessary when a cavalcade of familiar friendlies poured into view at the far end of the street, greeting him with hoots and howls of applause when they sighted the enemy dead.

It was to be ten years before Halliday heard of his saviour again.

Halliday drew the straight-back razor smoothly through the creamy lather along his powerful jaw-line then glided upwards fractionally, stopping when the blade reached the powerful mustache. He exam-

13

ined the results. Satisfied, he rinsed the razor, used a white hand towel to mop up what was left of the foam. When he was through he massaged his jaw then leaned forward a little to make an almost detached scrutiny of what a decade had done to his appearance.

What he saw was a big bronzed man of thirty with a crop of wavy dark hair and a full mustache that was almost black. Halliday could make his dark eyes twinkle when he chose, but it didn't seem worth the effort when there was nobody around. Stripped to the waist, he noted that ten years of hard living had not added any extra inches. Only scars. Of these he had any number, a couple as legacy of the war but the majority collected over the turbulent years since as he followed various career paths, most of them dangerous and all exciting to a greater or lesser degree.

This man craved excitement like a dog-wolf craves red meat. It was about the only honest to god addiction he had, he told to his bronzed image. But of course he lied. He had another which was just as powerful and demanding. But having just spent the past twenty-four hours sharing a high old time with the new dancer from the Forty Thieves Saloon, romance was not at that particular moment a paramount consideration.

He was about to say goodbye to Jilly. He didn't believe in long attachments, especially since Clara Cable had broken it off with him three days earlier, accusing him of being incapable of giving up what she termed his 'old wild ways'. His ranch hand out at the spread had told him he would be a fool to throw a girl like that over, just for the sake of a little excitement and 'fun'. But what would a half loco Mexican vaquero like Teo Caraso know about morality?

Halliday ran a brush over his hair and tweaked his mustache, then took a sip of whiskey from a flask in the stand. He liked the rare leisurely moments in life when he could pamper himself and take his time, a luxury often denied him as he plied his trade, whatever that trade might be. He wasn't sure if anyone had figured out a name for someone who ostensibly raised horses for a living, yet was prone to break off and take on just about any line of work at a moment's notice, providing only that it wasn't boring.

He met his gaze in the mirror, sober and contemplative now. Those two gunmen had jolted him and he had to admit it.

Colonel Dabney! How was that for a name out of the past!

He told himself he should feel pleased that a man to whom he owed his very life should have made contact after all this time. Hell! He was pleased! Yet something uneasy nagged at the edges of his mind whenever he thought about that Atlanta night. He only wished he could put a name to it.

With a sigh he turned away and padded across the good Brussels carpet to the bureau containing his clothes. Most times the Halliday wardrobe consisted of black shirt and hat, well worn Levis and a double gunrig. Working gear. But before retiring to the spread this last time he'd acquired a few refinements such as a pair of twill trousers, three new shirts including a pink one which aroused some interest on the streets, and a fine suede jacket which looked raffish but probably would not last a week out on the trail.

He reached for the pink shirt and accidentally brushed his gun belt, knocking it to the floor.

Halliday glanced at the bedroom door. He hated goodbyes. He'd planned to leave Jilly sleeping, slip into something flash, leave a brief note, maybe, and just disappear from her little life.

So much for the best laid plans.

The door opened and the Forty Thieves' main attraction stood there in her doorway wearing a sleepy smile and a blue-green bath towel.

'Darling,' she murmured, 'what are you doing?'

'Er, just have to go down to the lobby, sugar face. Go back to bed and I'll—'

'Darling,' she interrupted.

He wasn't quite sure he liked the smoky look in her eye. 'Yeah?'

She crooked a finger. 'What can you get in the lobby that you can't get here?'

Normally Halliday liked that kind of talk. Encouraged it even. But this was no normal situation. He really did have something to tend to in the lobby. And besides – twenty-four hours straight?

'Er . . . umm . . .'

'Buck honey, you sound almost bashful.' She pouted prettily, drawing the skimpy towel up beneath her dimpled chin, which naturally extended the exposure of her long dancer's legs. 'Or am I being naïve? Could it be you've just lost interest in little old me?'

16

This was a tough question. Halliday could remember the old days when, all alone and far from home away out on the Texas Panhandle, or three parts lost down the Grand Canyon hunting some backshooter or another, he would gladly have given an arm and maybe a leg for a vision like this to appear by his lonesome camp-fire.

But that was then; this was now, and now was different.

He put on his phoniest grin. 'Jilly, I'm not connin', honest. I've got two geezers downstairs who have serious business with me. Geezers with great manners and eyes like augers. Geezers who won't take no for an answer and . . .'

His flow of words just dried up in his throat as that blue-green bath towel slipped to the floor and his resolve was but a memory as he stepped through the doorway faster than she could say, 'Baby, you're just incredible.'

He knew it. But that didn't stop him setting out to prove it. Yet again, just for old times' sake.

Later, after he'd dressed leisurely and sat sprawled in a plush bedside chair holding her hand and puffing on a black cheroot, the man from the Circle H drowsily watched Jilly sleeping like a baby, her pretty blonde head filled with dreams of singing for presidents and kings.

Suddenly he realized his vision was playing him up.

Leastwise that was his first reaction as, gazing over Jilly's shoulder he suddenly saw two heads, heads so alike indeed that they might have been twins. Clean shaven and sternly sober young heads they were, surmounting starched white collars, neatly knotted bandannas, and guns. Each man wore a heavy caliber revolver on his hip beneath his sober jacket and they moved with the effortless grace of athletes as they moved round to the end of the bed.

Petrie and Cole had entered the locked suite without permission and now had the gall to shoot reproving stares at him and the sleeping woman!

In an instant he was on his feet. He squeezed Jilly's hand to alert her they no longer had the room to themselves, then made a lunge for his double gunrig hanging off of the bedhead.

Jilly jolted awake and screamed as the taller of the pair moved lightning fast to clamp a kid-gloved hand over Halliday's right wrist.

'Shoot them, baby!' she urged. 'This is the goddamn United States of America. People can't bust in on other people like that here in—'

'Shut up, baby.'

Halliday's tone was resigned. He was now sober, clear headed and fully alert. Plainly he'd underestimated the men he'd met earlier. He had certainly never figured they'd have the brass bound nerve to invade his privacy this way.

He was mad but it was controlled. For these men, and this intrusion were linked to a man he owed. That made everything very different.

The pair surveying him reprovingly resembled bank clerks or clever accountants on the way up, if you overlooked the eyes and the guns. They showed no perceptible interest in Jilly, which he might have thought a tad odd at another time. The short fair one, Cole, was reproving as he spoke.

'You gave us your word, Mr Halliday.'

'Down by ten, you promised,' supported the other.

'The colonel insisted we shouldn't have any trouble with you.'

'Said you owed him and that you were a man of honour who would recognize that fact and comply with—'

'All right – all goddamn right!' Halliday said testily, brushing the restraining hand aside and rose. He towered inches above them and spread his shoulders to emphasize his superior size. This could intimidate would-be troublemakers but these two simply stared up at him poker-faced and didn't budge an inch. They weren't afraid of him, and certainly had him on the griddle when they spoke of honor. His was a strange brand of honor many might find extremely flexible in some areas, non-existent in others. But by the same morality by which Buck Halliday would surely kill any man who tried to kill him, should anyone do him a great service, he considered himself in that man's debt until the debt was repaid. Even if that opportunity didn't arise until years on.

Following their first meeting he'd checked out their credentials as employees of the colonel and understood only too clearly what was being asked – demanded of him. He'd decided to give himself time to think things over, but Jilly had distracted him. He was thinking clearly now; thinking he'd like to bust Petrie one and upend Cole, but knew he wouldn't.

Well, he was almost sure.

Jilly was a hard woman to scare. After her initial outburst she'd quickly calmed and now seemed to find the situation amusing. She'd always regarded Halliday as a dangerous man underneath. It gave her pleasure to tame him in her own way, and she was intrigued by the notion that the two immaculate young strangers – whom she also intuitively saw as dangerous – seemed to hold some power or influence over the hero of Phoenix Crossing. Enshrouded modestly in the bed linen now, she sat with knees up to her chin and stared up at him with a questioning look that only made her look prettier.

He sighed for a second time and said, 'I won't even try to explain, honey, but I've gotta go.'

'Where to?' she sulked.

'Would you believe Wichita, Kansas?'

'That's enough,' warned the taller one, while the other touched his finger to his lips.

'Are they law?' Jilly queried.

'I'm not sure what they are,' Halliday replied, going to the door. 'But it doesn't make any difference. *Hasta*, baby.'

'Buck.'

'What?'

She wasn't sulking any longer. Her mood was worldly-wise now. 'Why don't you shake those two and get yourself back to Clara? You know you want to, and so do I, strangely enough.'

'Maybe I wish I could.'

'Hell, baby, I always thought Buck Halliday did whatever he wanted when he wanted. Don't tell me you're scared of these striplings?'

'That'll be the day.'

The three quit the rooms, the young guns from Wichita studying Halliday curiously as they took the stairs down.

'What did she mean by those remarks about the other woman, Mr Halliday?' he was asked. 'Isn't she your girlfriend?'

Halliday offered no reply. His mind was reaching ahead to Kansas and the man who was literally demanding he come visit with him. Nobody ever demanded anything from Buck Halliday. But Colonel Ketchell Dabney was anything but a nobody.

CHAPTER 2

MEET ME IN WICHITA

Viewed from the street, the place didn't look much, simply a sprawling collection of buildings well past their prime standing on a broad and dusty back street of Wichita about a block south of the railroad depot.

Halliday didn't realize they'd reached their destination until his escorts turned through the sagging gateway. He followed astride the barrel-chested dun, hat tipped to the back of his head and eyes playing over wagon sheds, barns, hayloft, outbuildings and sheds which clustered without apparent pattern about a dull brown building with pigeons on the roof and a worn old sign out front which read 'Wichita Feed And Grain'.

One glance told Halliday that the Wichita Feed And Grain played host to men afoot, on horseback and in light rigs, yet there was no sign of freighters or wagons such as one might expect.

He felt his escorts' eyes on him as he approached the hitchrack. He refused to show any hint of curiosity. For one reason, he doubted he could expect any straight answers from this pair. For another, ever since Arkansas, he'd been playing out the role as the silent hard man. He played it very well, for Buck Halliday could be silent and harder than most anybody when in the mood, and he was in that mood today.

He owed Colonel Dabney and admitted it. Yet this peremptory summons coming out of the blue almost a decade since they'd last crossed trails had resurrected that strange feeling of unease he'd experienced at the time of their meeting in burning Atlanta, which he had still.

Dabney had courageously saved his life, no doubt about that. But something in the manner the man had gone about it, watching his plight that night for some time until certain his attackers were out of bullets, then coming in to mow them down with every sign of enjoyment, had left a lingering odd taste in the mouth somehow.

Or could it be that he was simply resentful that a hand should reach out of the past that way to claim him after all those years? That was most likely, he decided, stepping down. And yet overlaying his resentment was his curiosity as he stood gazing up at the food and grain establishment which was plainly nothing of the kind. Dabney had always had the reputation as something of a remote and arrogant one back in the war days. He supposed it would be interesting to see if he'd changed any.

Petrie led the way in, Cole walking in back of Halliday. Halliday halted and motioned the fair-headed man ahead.

'Don't be difficult, sir,' Petrie warned. 'You've been surprisingly co-operative since Arkansas, despite the fact that the colonel seemed to think you might prove recalcitrant. Don't spoil it.'

'This joint doesn't hit me right,' he growled. 'You walk ahead. Unless you want to see some A-grade recalcitrance, that is?'

The pair traded looks. They shrugged inside their tailored black coats. Cole stepped past Halliday and the trio continued down a musty corridor to where a man the size of a small shed lounged against a counter, huge feet rammed into boots resembling howitzer casings.

'Mr Halliday to see Mr Dabney,' the escorts stated, and the man-mountain grunted and opened a big old steel door that was painted puke green where it wasn't rusting away.

They went through and Halliday propped. He stood in a carpeted lobby illuminated by skylights. In the center of the lobby stood an impressive reception desk attended by men shaved, attired and presented in much the same way as were Petrie and Cole.

Passageways ran off the lobby like the spokes of a half wheel, and he glimpsed more smartly-attired people coming and going, all quietly purposeful, moving in and out of various rooms on what certainly appeared to be important business.

He scratched the back of his neck. He'd once visited a highly respectable law firm in Chicago, and this was the closest set-up he'd seen to it since. But the firm of Clayton, Clayton and Grimshaw had looked like a law firm from outside, not a run down feed and grain outfit.

In silence he was taken through to an inner chamber where two men in sober suits guarded an oaken door. He passed through and found himself in the presence of former Colonel Dabney, who was rising from an overstuffed swivel chair behind a splendid mahogany desk. He was a quick-moving impressive man with steel-colored eyes who appeared to have been dealt with kindly by the years. The welcoming smile was as empty as Halliday remembered, but the handshake was firm and strong, the voice cultivated and warm.

'Lieutenant Halliday. My total gratitude for your responding so readily to my cry for help.'

'Is that what it was?' Halliday replied guardedly. 'The twins didn't say.'

'The twins?'

Halliday jerked a thumb over his shoulder. 'The look-alikes. It's a little like seeing double, wouldn't you say?'

Dabney just grunted and motioned the gunmen out, leaving the two alone.

Halliday appreciated the fact that Dabney immediately got down to cases once both had glasses of Kentucky Gold whiskey in hand.

The big man was in the security business, he learned. The Wichita Feed And Grain was the cover for Western Investigation Bureau, an organization which worked for all sorts of people, principally state and federal governmental departments and ancillaries. The bureau's activities stretched far and wide, and recently had found itself called upon to investigate a suspect operation in South Dakota which might or might not be involved in certain illegal activities taking place in the Black Hills.

Dabney paused to sip his whiskey. Halliday lighted up a powerful golden cigar. He waited. They were alone yet he sensed people close by. He noticed a slight tic in his host's clean-shaven cheek. An expensive clock on the wall chimed the quarter hour and Dabney resumed his narrative, hunching his shoulders and rolling his glass smoothly between his palms as he spoke. He gave the impression he was coming to the crux of his story, which proved to be the case.

'I shall make it brief and plain, Buckley,' he said quietly. 'Prior to our dramatic meeting in Georgia all that time ago, I was involved in a particular incident during the Battle of Vicksburg during which I lost a company of some forty men during an enemy counter attack. I afterwards discovered there was one survivor, a certain Major Cunningham who was left crippled in the battle and hitherto played no further part in the hostilities. Er, your drink need freshening?'

'It's fine.'

Dabney leaned back, dark eyes brooding.

'This officer held a grudge against me and made certain scurrilous allegations which he was of course unable to substantiate. Before vanishing into civilian life post-war he made certain threats against me which I treated with the contempt they warranted.

You can imagine my surprise when my agents working in the Dakotas turned up the name of former
Major Cunningham as being heavily involved in
highly suspect and possibly treasonous activities.'

'Is he the one you want me to kill?'

Dabney appeared startled.

'What?'

Halliday set his glass down on the desk top.

'Colonel, I worked for security intelligence on
both sides of the trenches during the war, as I reckon
you'd know full well. You'd also have to know I've
handled plenty assignments for the government in
the years since, though I've just about phased them
out of my life now. We both know most of it is dirty
work, you know, the kind most men don't want to
take on. I've sat across any number of desks from
men in 'security' who wanted someone arrested,
someone warned off – often someone killed. Those
men always had a certain look about them, and
you've got it stamped all over you. So, I'll ask again,
is Cunningham the geezer you want killed in return
for your savin' my life in Atlanta?'

It was a long taut moment before Dabney let a
held breath go.

'You're a remarkable man, Mr Halliday, hard,
intelligent and perceptive.'

'Let's skip the bullshit. Is he or ain't he?'

Halliday spoke harshly, and felt that way.

'Yes. My agents unfortunately were unable to
conceal their connections with me when they made
contact with Cunningham's people up there, and
they discovered that the man, obviously crazed, has

been searching for me without success with revenge in mind almost since the war's end. He intends to murder me, Mr Halliday, and I'm not at all sure that this organization I have here can stop him, judging from what I've learned of his strength and his nature. Can you believe such people exist?'

Halliday's face was grim. He hated it, yet knew he would do it. A man lived by a certain code. If he didn't he wasn't much of a man. But before he committed himself there were some things he needed to know, some out of simple curiosity, others in the interest of survival. On the surface, Operation Badlands sounded dangerous enough even by his standards.

He lighted a cigar, Dabney following his every move. Halliday's eyes were hazed by smoke as he spoke.

'Are you tellin' me everythin' about why he wants to kill you so bad, ten years on?'

'All you need to know.'

This was flashback stuff to the days when Dabney was a full colonel of cavalry, Halliday just a junior officer. Halliday almost smiled behind his tobacco smoke camouflage. They never changed, not even when they wanted you to do something for them real bad. Some people couldn't change. He suspected he was one of them.

He screwed his big head towards the door. His hearing was acute. Someone was out there, real close.

He said, 'Just what sort of outfit is this anyway? The two you sent to fetch me, the men I see here. Know what they look like to me?'

'What?'

'Federal agents is what. But they ain't, are they?'

'You're perceptive, as I said, Mr Halliday. No, they are certainly not Federal personnel, but I train them like them and often the work they do for the bureau is similar. Without exception they are tough, highly trained personnel who get results in any task I assign them.'

'Even gun jobs?'

'Why do you ask?'

Halliday flicked gray ash into a heavy brass tray. 'Doesn't it stick out a mile, man?' He gestured. 'Here you are, operatin' an outfit that employs dangerous lookin' geezers in numbers, you've got a problem, yet instead of just siccin' your own people onto this man you claim wants to rub you out, you go to all sorts of trouble to round me up. Why not them? Why not put my escorts on the job? They ain't got any sense of humor but they seem tough enough.'

'For one simple reason. I want Cunningham killed, not just scared off or tipped off. And because of his isolation and the strength surrounding the man, I doubt very much that any strength of numbers I might put into the field against him could achieve either stealth or success. In short, this is a task for one trained killer, and seeing as I helped train you, Lieutenant, I know you're qualified. Now, anything else?'

'Guy lives through hell and gone up to the badlands . . .' Halliday mused, drawing deep. 'Successful, maybe crooked, crippled, protected,

maybe loco, out to kill you ten years after the war.
Sounds dangerous enough to me.'

'Will you do it?'

Halliday had known all along what his answer
would be.

'If I do, we're square,' he said.

Dabney's face flooded with relief.

'I knew I could rely on you,' he said emotionally.
He leaned forward intensely. 'But I must warn you,
Lieutenant, it will not be easy.'

'Murder rarely is,' Halliday said darkly. Then
added with a touch of cold irony, 'Even when it's in a
good cause.'

The simple people of Federal Street, Wichita, were
long accustomed to the strange goings on at Wichita
Feed And Grain. Men arrived and left at all hours of
the day and night and virtually none looked like he
knew anything more about stock feed than he did
about cowboying.

Yet it was interesting to watch them come and go,
and now and again there was an incident or perhaps
a visitor to the place which drew them to their
windows in numbers to watch and speculate and ask
that hackneyed question of another: 'Just exactly
what do they do in there anyhow?'

The big rider on the dun horse who rode out of
the yard just on dusk that night was definitely worth
a second look. From the crown of his flat-brimmed
hat to the heels of his heavy range boots, he looked
like trouble of the interesting kind as he turned his
broad back on the depot yard and headed uptown.

Curtains were let drop and faces moved back from windows when the watchers realized that two regulars from the mystery establishment had emerged in the dusk also to watch the big rider's departure. It was not that those young, clean-shaven men in their neat dark clothing bothered the citizens of Federal Street. They didn't. Yet there was something about them that made people cautious just the same.

Cole and Petrie paid no attention to the houses; their attention was on the receding figure in the dying light.

'What do you think?'

'The colonel believes he can do it.'

'He's undisciplined.'

'His record's impressive.'

'I smell a loose cannon.'

'What bothers me, if you want to know the truth, is that if Halliday fails, the colonel's going to have to send us after Cunningham.'

'Isn't that what we're trained for?'

'Cunningham's not like anyone else we've come up against. I guess I'd sooner be in hell with a bad back than heading in there. We don't even know how many he's got there in the badlands.'

'You sound as if you're having doubts Halliday will get it done now.'

'No, the colonel reckons he's up to it so that's good enough for me.'

'You ever seen Dabney scared before, Cole?'

'That's treason talk, Petrie. Come on, we need a drink. We'll toast Halliday's luck.'

'In that case, better make it two drinks.'

ONE LAST NOTCH

*

An endless trail. A man starts out at one place and
rides for the far horizon. But he can't get to where
he'd heading without using his guns – on the fron-
tier, in the war, bossing the wagon trains. And just
when he figures he might be able to see trail's end,
someone's shoving a gun in his fist again and he
knows he's got to use it . . . knows that maybe the trail
doesn't have an ending after all. Just rolls on forever,
as dark as the night and as long as Eternity. . . .

Halliday raised his glass in the gloom of the
balcony and stared at nothing. It was bitter whiskey
he was drinking. Times like this, whiskey was about
all a man had.

CHAPTER 3

BADLANDS

Halliday halted to listen to the wind. It came moaning soft and low out of a nameless watercourse off to his right to stir his mustache and hum along his hatbrim.

Then it was still again.

The badlands were like that: strange, different and unpredictable.

For a moment he thought of his horse, snug and comfortable ten miles back in a trailhouse livery, likely munching corn and starting to doze a little. Being a typical westerner, he would rather ride a hundred miles than walk ten, but this job and this terrain put riding out of the question. So that big loafing dun dozed and fed its face while its master wore out his boot leather as he drove deeper and deeper into a landscape as strange and alien as the backside of the moon.

And thinking momentarily of the horse as he

rested up a minute, his thoughts flickered to another sometime travelling companion whom he hadn't sighted in months and whom he didn't miss one little bit. So far as sidekicks went, he rated Caraso as about a one on a scale of ten. He was missing his horse at the moment, but that bow-legged Mexican horse thief? Not a bit.

He scratched his jaw and frowned. It was always a risk, leaving the Mex in charge at the spread. Sure, he could take care of the stock better than any man living. But that didn't say he was reliable. He didn't know how long this job would take him. . . .

He shook his head. The hell with that! He would do what he must and get back there just as fast as he might.

He concentrated on the next fissure, the next series of strangely shaped hummocks and the possibility of the next sighting.

He'd sighted them twice during the long day, distant figures on horseback making their way through this twisted chunk of South Dakota real estate as though they were part of it. They could be Indians, he mused, or maybe something even more alien.

Halliday inhaled.

What could possess a man to set up in a land like this voluntarily, if indeed that was what Cunningham had done?

He supposed he might find out if he succeeded in reaching the Fort without getting his head shot off.

The map and details he'd been supplied with back in Wichita were sketchy. The Bureau people who'd reconnoitred here had pin-pointed Cunningham's headquarters at roughly ten miles north by north-west of the spot where he now stood. They named it the 'Fort' as they claimed that was what it resembled from a distance, a solid looking edifice strategically placed on high ground above a badlands stream.

On that patrol, Dabney's scouts had not gotten anywhere close before being set upon by horsemen who left two Bureau hands dead and one taken captive.

It appeared that it had been from that hostage that Cunningham had learned about the Bureau and its leader, thus accidentally getting a lead on the hated Dabney whom he was said to have been hunting ever since the war.

Too bad, Halliday mused. But for a chance happening, Cunningham might have been still content with whatever strange business that had kept him amused up here, while Buck Halliday might well be still in Arkansas working his horses and keeping out of trouble, for a change.

He started off, a long striding figure with eyes probing the hazing twilight.

All this was regarded as Cunningham country now, so he'd been informed. His by right of might. As far as a man could see, wastelands, gully-washes, gaunt buttes and mysterious distances – all of it. He envisioned it in the form of circles within circles, like a shooting target, focusing down to the Fort, the center of it all. The fount of power. The home and castle of the man he'd come to kill.

He dismissed the image and concentrated exclusively upon the next yard, the next rise, the imperative of sighting the enemy before he was sighted. For secrecy and stealth would be his prime weapons here; he must thread his way through those circles of danger before positioning himself to hammer a bullet through Cunningham's head and so resolve his debt of honour to the man who had once saved his life.

Halliday travelled light. Two sixguns, a Bowie, a sneak two-shot behind a big silver belt buckle, a pint whiskey flask filled with spring water and some chocolate. At midnight he crawled into some brush and slept with one eye open and his hand on his gun.

Halliday had slept in some strange places with some strange people, like Jilly. But this was dramatically different from any hilltop bordello in Old Mexico, any mountain man's shack in the blizzard-ripped Judith Basin or aboard a storm-tossed trawler crossing the Great Lakes.

The badlands were a freak of nature, a region of severe erosion characterized by countless gullies, steep ridges and sparse vegetation. Here over the centuries, heavy rains had pounded poorly cemented sediments that had few deep-rooted plants to hold them together. Depressions gradually deepened into gullies and gullies could become great ugly gashes and ravines. By night particularly it was a place where it was easy enough to envision phantoms, ogres and the undead prowling about: that's if you had that type of imagination.

Halliday didn't.

On a dangerous assignment he was as uncomplicated as a piston engine. He was part of the savage land and at least as dangerous as anything crawling over its tortured surface that night.

When he woke it was daylight. He munched some chocolate, rinsing his mouth with water before swallowing it, attended his personal needs then crawled up a saddle-shaped rise to study the landscape before moving on.

No cigars. He well knew just how far the tang of tobacco smoke could travel in the outdoors. He left no tang or no tracks. He was a lethal force probing deep into danger territory, focused and committed. Get there, kill, get out. Simple if you said it quick.

The land lay silent in the sunlight. Halliday studied the sun and set his course before dropping back into the gullywashes and striking north.

He travelled very fast now, covering the earth in a crouching run that soon had him bathed in sweat. His breathing was normal after one mile, after five. He was in the prime of his years and in peak physical condition. The sun zenithed and slid down the sky. Ten miles as the crow flew became many more due to the necessity of clinging to the gullies to avoid detection. He paused briefly for water and chocolate, aching for a Cuban, swabbed his face off on his sleeve and jogged on.

He deliberately thought of burning Atlanta. He'd been a dead-set dead man when Dabney showed up with his killing guns. This was his motivation and it was a good one.

Mid-afternoon saw him belly his way up another sparsely-grassed bulge which commanded a wide view.

He immediately ducked his head and tugged off his hat. Less than a mile away, riders were appearing and disappearing as they followed the contours of a broken-backed ridge.

He counted nine; four whites, three Indians and two Orientals. Near as he could figure they were heading due east, possibly making for the Black Hills.

He fingered his mustache.

The Black Hills were emerging as something of a hot spot as a result of Custer discovering gold there, since when it had become impossible to prevent white miners invading the hills in defiance of treaties with the Sioux. Reading between the lines of what he had seen and heard in Wichita, Halliday believed Dabney to be deeply involved in what was going on out there and had a hunch it could have been an overlapping interest in the Black Hills of both Dabney and Cunningham that resulted in each becoming suddenly aware of the other's threatening presence.

Both were grabbers, he speculated. He knew the breed well. Always there were big men in the West eager to sweep riches into their fists, greedy, driven men for whom suddenly the marks of success were huge ranches, cattle kingdoms, railroads, mines, property, people, votes.

He scorned them all. His was a different hunger. Halliday enjoyed women and big money and high times, but most of all, lusted for excitement. It was the one thing which prevented his growing cynical, world-weary, or worst of all, bored.

He wasn't feeling bored at all as he watched those horsemen shrink first into blobs, then mere dots and finally invisibility, before turning his gaze northwards to see it standing there in the distance, its mud walls daubed by the lowering sun.

The Fort.

'Lousy beans,' grunted Sergei.

'Who eats beans?' commented Abilene.

The giant continued eating as Abilene blew perfect smoke rings at the ceiling. Whereas the foot soldiers of the private army here in the heart of the badlands ate in the mess off the horse yards within the walls of the Fort, Major Cunningham's top *segundos* enjoyed the run of the place and could eat wherever they pleased.

Today Sergei chose the small dining-room off the galley, which was operated by a smooth-skinned Chinese woman, a cousin of Cunningham's mistress, Lu Nin.

Of Russian extraction but raised in America, Sergei was the biggest man in the badlands with an appetite to match. Eye-patched, scarred and formidable in every way that counted, the big man put a sly look on his partner as his big thick teeth mashed a jawful of beans into pulp.

'How come you lose your appetite when you're nervous, Ab?'

'Who's nervous?'

'You've been jittery all week.'

'And why would that be so, Large Ass?' Abilene's tone was testy. At just a little over one-forty pounds, dagger-slim, vain and as arrogant as a flamenco dancer, he was the most dangerous man at the Fort, ergo the badlands. Afraid of nothing and always ready to prove it, this gentleman of the gun was swift to react to any implied doubt on the subject of his courage.

'Could have something to do with what's been going on.'

'Nothing's been going on.'

Sergei paused, spoon halfway to his mouth. 'That's just the point. Nothing. Nothing doing. Yet the major has been expecting trouble every minute. That's what's been eating on your liver, mister. Mine too. He's had us on full alert ever since we tangled with those Bureau reps from Kansas, but there's been nothing to see. That's got him jittery first, and now me and you.'

Abilene rose and moved restlessly to a window overlooking the wide yards around which the Fort was built. Through these yards passed the personnel, the wagons and all the goods of trade which drove and financed their employer's enterprises. Post-war, Major Cunningham overcame crippling disabilities to make his mark in the West, trading, dealing, supplying hard-to-get commodities both legal and the illicit kind. By the time he was in a position to consolidate and set himself up in real strength at a geographical location which would appeal to few men of means, Cunningham was able to indulge himself insofar as such things as creature comforts, personnel and pandering to his many idiosyncrasies were concerned.

The head man here had power, money and charisma which attracted others to work for him, follow him, and give their loyalty.

Abilene was a cold killer who loved this alien and hostile land. He took an active leadership role in the more daring and risky of the many Cunningham enterprises, and along with Sergei held himself responsible for the boss man's personal safety.

But of course the big man was right about the mood here. The men of the gun were edgy. Full alert for weeks – and nothing. Yet Cunningham insisted that Dabney – a personal enemy and a man of intense hatred and quiet conscience – was capable of brutal and immediate action without warning, and that he had reason to believe he might strike their organization at any moment.

During those weeks just about every man at the Fort had been on full alert and waiting for what might prove to be their greatest threat since they'd fought and defeated a bunch of renegade Indians who'd violently challenged their usurping of their badlands a year earlier.

Waiting, so Abilene believed, could be tougher on a man than going to the mat with the most dangerous enemy in their murky, violent business.

Dusk was settling as the gunman's brooding eye played restlessly over stockade, storehouse, turret, gate-house, armoury, living quarters and corrals, until his gaze finally focused upon Devil.

The ugly, swivel-hipped wild horse was Cunningham's particular pet, a critter so mean it had to be housed in its own corral, so fastidious that it would only accept feed from Cunningham's hand, and mean-spirited to such a degree that even the stoic Sioux and phlegmatic Chinese amongst the self-named 'Avengers' gave it a wide berth.

More than once, after sustaining a kick or bite from the the animal, Abilene had shoved a silver Colt through the rails of the corral, cocked the hammer and drawn a bead on the ragged blaze running down the center of Devil's ugly face. But he never pulled trigger.

The major would go loco if he did, and he'd seen the boss man in one of his rare loco moods. Scary – even for a top gun.

Sergei was saying something about the party which had left for the Black Hills that morning, but Abilene did not reply.

He was watching the wild mustang curiously.

The horse stood stock still in the center of its yard, facing the west where the sun was burning out like an old fire. Its ears were pricked and the scrubby tail was lifted. Never even remotely prepossessing, Devil looked even uglier than normal with its long Roman nose crinkling as it raised and lowered its head in a series of little jerky motions that would seem to have nothing to do with anything, unless you knew the critter as Abilene did.

Cunningham boasted that his mount was the finest watchdog here or anyplace else. Abilene agreed with this. Which was why he suddenly reacted with a stiffening of his spine and a quick pivoting of his sleek head when he saw how the half-wild critter was acting up. He knew instantly that the animal had seen, sensed or scented something alien in this on-drawing badlands night.

Abilene cut his gaze up to the parapets where sentries paced slowly to and fro. Plainly they had not seen anything. So whose instincts did he trust, a wild horse's or the sentries'?

The answer revealed itself as he drew his Colt, span nimbly away from the windows and hissed, 'Let's go!' to a startled Sergei, then vanished down the passageway leading to the western door. 'All hands on full alert – now!'

'What the hell are we gettin' excited about?' Sergei bellowed after him.

'He smells someone unfamiliar, damnit!'

The big man tipped the last of his beans down his throat, belched and followed at a lumbering trot.

Halliday scratched his temple with the foresights of his Colt .45.

Before him in the dying light lay the Fort. Cunningham's citadel. It loomed before him in the soft night, all ghostly and strange at close quarters with high slab walls and brooding watchtowers. The heavy stockade gates only needed to have a draw-bridge and moat installed to complete the picture of some outpost lifted from the Old World with little connection to the American West.

Sprawled in the man-sized fissure where he'd lain unmoving, unseen and as patient as a hostile for several hours, Halliday looked at the sky.

Soon it would be dark.

He drew a big breath down deep into his lungs.

Everything else up to this point had been routine, regulation scouting stuff involving technique, trailsmanship and just plain common sense such as he had employed many times before in so many places. Now the tempo changed. No point in waiting for Cunningham to show himself outside his walls, he figured. The man was a cripple who only rarely ventured abroad. Halliday knew he would have to go in, even though his rough estimates of enemy strength varied from between twenty and forty.

If there was one thing he was not short of out here, it was odds-against.

Yet he was cool as he waited for the final dying of the light. He was a professional, he'd played these deadly games countless times before, his allies would be darkness and the inestimable benefit of surprise.

Or so he believed, and why should he think otherwise?

His head jerked up. An iron-hinged wooden gate set in the west wall creaked open and a figure slouched out, making for the pumphouse which sucked up water from the creek to the Fort.

The opportunity he'd been waiting for?

Stalking the man, Halliday was a wraith, a ghost and a silent phantom. His plan was as uncomplicated as a Bowie knife. Take the man out, disguise himself in his rig, saunter back inside – and Dabney could order a sympathy wreath for a respected enemy.

He closed in. The man was fiddling with the pump engine, whistling through his teeth. Halliday was in the act of raising his Colt overhead prior to bringing it down hard on a blocky head, when a close voice touched him like ice.

'Freeze or you're dead, you son of a bitch!'

He swung around tigerishly, sixgun levelled, finger tightening, ready to hurl himself flat and cut loose. To fight. To kill.

'We got you cold,' a second voice, equally menacing, spoke from directly behind him. 'We've been expecting you along for almost an hour, pilgrim. Better take his guns before he does something dumb and we have to blow him apart, Tanner.'

The man at the pump came forward. Halliday could make out the crouched figures crouching in the deep pump ditch now. They were well positioned, professionally so. It was like they'd known he was coming. But how could that be so? He was a pro . . . wasn't he?

'Your guns, pilgrim!'

They were growing impatient. He had but two options. He could start shooting and die, or do the other thing.

He stood stock still and let the man take his guns. The other two closed in, a giant with yard-wide shoulders and a slim man of the all-too-familiar gunman breed.

'Well, looks like we caught the real McCoy,' the smaller man said, looking him over. 'No tiddler this one, eh, Sergei?'

'Barracuda,' affirmed the giant, ramming his gun in Halliday's ribs. 'Move, big fish.'

Halliday moved.

CHAPTER 4

TOUGH ENOUGH

Halliday had a trick he employed at times like this. He went traveling. No, not in actuality. Real, honest to God traveling wasn't on the agenda when you happened to find yourself trussed up hand and foot and encircled by unsmiling heavies taking it in turns to smash you in the face. It was all in the mind, and as Sergei's big fist slammed into his jaw, causing sweat and blood to fly again, he finally settled on a destination.

Only one place appealed.

San Clemente, Mexico.

Yes.

Strumming guitars, endless sunshine, no work to speak of, dissolute men who still could fight, dark-eyed woman waiting for the night and lovers.

Carmelita.

He wanted to believe she might still be waiting for him even though he'd dumped her for a rich widow whose husband had made his money in surgical trusses.

He was certain she hadn't forgotten him.

People didn't forget Buck Halliday.

Or miss him either, he was forced to reflect as visions of sleepy San Clemente faded under the impact of a blow that jarred his brain and maybe loosened a tooth.

He stared up into the glistening face of Sergei. He was figuring the spots he could hit this heavyweight which would either cripple or kill. They'd taught him all the murderous tricks during the war, and it wasn't something a man forgot. Too bad about the thongs, though. And there was no overlooking the motley crew of white men, Indians and Chinese watching Sergei working on him either.

He sensed he'd surrendered his life the moment he gobbled down the bait of that man coming outside the walls to the pump.

They meant to kill him. He could see it in their faces. He was sure he'd be dead now had he given them what they wished to know about him.

'Name.' Sergei was panting. He'd stripped to the waist. He had muscles on his muscles. Halliday was unimpressed. The breed he respected most was the man who could fill his hand with Colt faster than you could blink and was capable of hammering six slugs into a moving target shooting from the hip. Someone who was just as fast and deadly with the odds against him as when things were all his way.

He'd like to think that was the Halliday kind, for that was the breed he most admired. But right now he felt nothing like any kind of winner.

And wondered if he mightn't be turning light-headed as the blows continued to fall, until someone spoke quietly and Sergei stepped back.

Halliday saw three Abilenes, then two. He blinked and just one stood behind him, drawing soft kid gloves from fine hands. One was likely enough.

'You've got to be the dumbest one we ever caught,' he was told in a cold, mocking voice. 'You could be stone dead by now, should be, by rights. Yet you still don't have the brains to know we'll let up on you if you just answer two simple questions. Who are you? And who sent you? Simple.'

Halliday spat blood. He could sure use a Cuban cigarillo around about now.

Hell! He wouldn't even complain should a certain Mexican no-account come through that big double door staggering under the weight of a Gatling gun and shooting the living shit out of everything that moved. Should that unlikely event occur, why, he wouldn't even call down Teo Caraso for quitting the spread and leaving his horses to die of thirst. . . .

He forced his pain-addled brain to straighten itself up and did his level best to stare the man he'd heard called Abilene square in the eye.

'Open a vein,' he growled.

'You're a pro,' Abilene said in a matter-of-fact tone. 'Written all over you. The way you got through our lines. No identification on you. How you've made Sergei work for no results. Sure, Jack, you're a hired pro. But we need to know who by. I need to know, Major Cunningham is real keen to know. What have you got to lose?'

'Dead men tell no tales, gunslick.'

'What?'

'The only thing keeping me alive is your curiosity. Once you learn what you want to know, I'm dead. Simple.'

'It was Dabney, wasn't it?'

'Never heard the name.'

'Has to be him. He knows we are going to kill him. We've been waiting for him to make his move ever since we got tangled up with his people, and and now you've made it. Where'd you leave your mount?'

'Up a tree.'

He expected the hammering to resume, but it didn't. Abilene murmured something to Sergei and both men went to stand in the doorway. Others lit up and sat around, watching Halliday like he had two heads.

Taking advantage of the breather, Halliday took sharp stock of his surroundings. They'd brought him to a large warehouse piled high with sacks, crates and stacks of weapons. He'd heard that the Black Hills Indians, Sioux mostly, were harassing the intruding miners with modern weapons, up to and including Winchester .32s. Just glancing around, he saw more of that brand of rifle than any other.

What did that mean?

And did he give a damn?

No way. It was just force of habit. As Abilene had said, he was a professional.

The day wore on. They gave him nothing to eat or

drink and by mid-afternoon it was stifling hot in the warehouse. Eventually he was taken outside and marched across the baking quadrangle to enter a cool, thick-walled building whose interior was as comfortable and immaculate as the finest hotel in Little Rock.

They ushered him into a room thickly carpeted but sparsely furnished. There was a maze of gleaming silver steel handrails. Rough hands lashed him to a chair which was already securely tethered to one of the waist-high handrails. Abilene spoke and the others left. The gunman opened a side door and a man rolled through in a wheelchair, staring at the prisoner curiously.

Cunningham was in his mid-forties, a man who had been handsome once before injury and illness overcame him. His hair was silver and his complexion pale, as though he rarely got out in the sun. The face was a curious blend of strength and weakness, determination and self-pity.

He shook his head at Abilene's offer to assist him from the chair. Somehow he managed to heave himself up between two parallel hand rails, which he gripped with fierce determination, useless legs swinging beneath him.

Thus supported, he swung slowly and painfully towards Halliday, whose battered face remained stony blank. If Halliday had any pity to spare he would lavish it on himself.

Cunningham finally halted, intense eyes probing. The man showed surprise. 'Army,' he stated.

'What?' Halliday said.

The man nodded to a relaxed Abilene. 'Written all over him, the carriage, the bearing, the strength of jaw, the defiance.' He cut his gaze back to Halliday. 'Military training . . . sticks with a man for life. Who were you with, soldier?'

'He won't talk,' said Abilene. He was right. Halliday was a Sphinx. Yet Cunningham didn't react as expected.

'I'll wager we have something on him in the files, Abilene. Go alert the staff and set them to work. Six-three or four, thirtyish, cavalry if I'm any guess.' He paused to run his eyes over Halliday's scarred and naked torso. 'Several woundings. Officer, of course, but a maverick or I'm a Dutchman. Have them check on courts martial, disciplinary hearings, that sort of thing.'

He stopped abruptly, snapping his fingers. 'Just a minute. Of course! Why am I so obtuse?'

Abilene paused in the doorway. 'What is it, Major?'

'The obvious, of course,' Cunningham replied. He thrust a finger at Halliday. 'You were with the 25th weren't you? That's why Dabney chose you. Of course he'd select someone he knew and could trust to do the job. What section were you in? Special Services? A commando, for certain. Well, man, there's nothing to be gained by your silence now. We both know I've uncovered you. Who are you?'

Halliday said nothing. Cunningham, growing impatient now, dispatched his man with added specific instructions to the File Room. Less than ten minutes elapsed before Abilene returned to hand Cunningham a slip of paper. The man scanned it, then smiled.

'Lieutenant Buckley Halliday, scout, special forces

and commando unit. By glory, Abilene, just look at
this record. This is no common garden backshooting
killer. This man is a hero. Isn't that so, Buckley?'

Halliday was weary of keeping his mouth shut. It
wasn't his style anyway.

'Sorry I can't say the same about you, Cunningham.
The hero bit, I mean.'

Cunningham's smile vanished. He heaved himself
closer, expression intent.

'I was never a coward, regardless of what that court
martial found. Dabney was the betrayer, the quitter
in the face of the enemy who had to blacken me to
save himself. . . .' He halted with an obvious effort.
The strained smile reappeared. 'He seduced you, of
course. Doubtless called on your old loyalty to
convince you that you should kill me for his good
and that of the country. You are a Dabney victim just
as much as I, Mr Halliday—'

He broke off, suddenly started to slump. Abilene
was quick with a chair. It took a minute for the man
to get his breath. He waved weakly with a limp hand.

'Place him in the brig for the moment. He's to
receive the very best of attention . . . no more punish-
ment. Ignoring our unfortunate start, Buck, I'm
quite sure we shall reach an understanding when you
learn the full truth about the colonel. Now . . . now
I'm very tired.'

So was Halliday. But he was not about to complain.
He was still alive, which was surely just about the last
thing he'd expected to be by the time this sick, fasci-
nating man was through with him today.

*

The mule bucked and the kid landed on his head.

It was an inevitable outcome, for the kid couldn't ride and Joachim was one of the most unpredictable mules on either side of the Big Muddy.

The scrawny Mexican checked out his mule first before looking to the bawling kid sitting in the hot dust of Topeka's Cross Street.

That was a mistake. A big one.

The mother caught him across the back of the neck with her furled parasol. Teo Caraso staggered three steps, grabbing at his neck and cursing in Spanish. She got him in the ribs next, ramming the point in as if she was a fencing instructor at an academy. He yowled and cursed in English and the overweight young matron belted him another on that score before clutching little Bobby to her bosom.

'Oh, my poor blossom. What did the horrible man do to you?' She focused on the mule. It was easy to hate Joachim. Even Caraso hated him, and he owned him. The Mexican was a horse thief and horse lover whose golden dream was one day to own his own huge rancho in Sonora stocked by milk white Arabian blood horses of impeccable lineage. In the meantime, he was journeying north on Joachim and in times of harsh economic necessity sold 'pony rides' on him to anyone stupid enough to be taken in by his sign. 'That . . . that thing should be shot!' she claimed. 'It's a menace to public safety . . . and so are you.'

Caraso was tired. He was disgusted. He was sick of the sound of her voice.

He swore at her in Spanish, then next moment

found himself being lifted off the ground by a resounding kick to the backside.

He whirled to confront the husky young man with a five-pointed star on his vest.

'I heard that, Mex. Apologize to Mrs Johnson, and I mean right now.'

Now Teo Caraso was no hero as anyone who knew him – such as employer Buck Halliday – would readily testify. Even so he was not entirely without a certain south-of-the-border brand of courage when called upon to dredge it up. For a moment he was weary and disillusioned enough to be tempted to tell the earnest young deputy what he could do and where he could go to do it.

But only for a moment.

He was a lone Mexican vaquero in the land of the gringo. If put to it, he might be able to whip one deputy, but never one deputy and an outraged American mother together. Even Halliday wouldn't take on that kind of a challenge.

So he apologized. He gave the woman back the dime she'd paid for the so-called pony ride. The woman told him to get back to Mexico and the deputy ordered him off his nice clean Topeka streets.

It was quiet under the bridge where he'd camped during his slow crossing of dusty Kansas. Seated on his bedroll, Teo Caraso was too dejected even to make coffee. He just sat there staring moodily at the slow flowing Republican River rolling by, shifted his weight to reach for his tobacco and felt the letter in his pocket.

He took it out and read:

I'm working for the man again.

Should be back in Arkansas in a couple of weeks or so.

Stay put. Work the horses. Don't get the wanders and don't drink.

The letter wasn't signed. There was no need. Nobody ever wrote to Teo Caraso but his employer and occasional trail partner, Buck Halliday.

He'd had the letter a week and had disregarded it almost from the moment he read it. For Halliday had a rare talent for trouble while his ranch hand had a totally exaggerated notion of his responsibilities to the man who'd somewhat offhandedly saved his skinny neck and reluctantly offered him a job on the Circle H ranch.

He knew Halliday was in big trouble up north – and what loyal hand wouldn't be ready to leave thirty or forty half-broken horses to fend for themselves to go bring a good man back safe and sound?

Halliday reckoned Teo Caraso was a little crazy. It was quite possible he was right. But the truth of it was, during their time on the ranch, the crafty Mexican had indeed helped drag his employer out of more than one tight spot through a combination of native intelligence, dedication and blind luck.

He might do so again, Caraso mused as he leaned back against the sturdy timbers of the Republican River Bridge, and smiled nostalgically, even a little wistfully. For had he not often remarked that the only reason he tolerated Halliday's heavy-handed ways, was the excitement?

It was really Halliday who was crazy; he was convinced of this. No man took so many mother-loving risks with his life, slipped under the covers with more dangerous women, antagonized powerful people in such numbers or lived closer to the edge than the big man who sometimes, condescendingly and patronizingly might refer to Teo Caraso as his sidekick.

Watching Halliday swagger through life and waiting to see just what really loco thing he might do next – before it all ended violently as he knew it one day must – had almost become this Mexican vagabond's main interest in life.

He knew Halliday would be enraged when he discovered he'd quit the spread, but he would surely also be grateful. In time he hoped.

He reflected on what he'd learned of the events surrounding the big man in Paradise prior to his hasty departure for the north. He scratched his head and wondered if he was worrying too much about Halliday leaving in a hurry with two dangerous looking strangers without telling a soul where he was going or why.

He decided he wasn't, and within twenty minutes was astride with his cranky mule's ugly nose pointed towards South Dakota. He hoped he could trust the person who'd offered to keep an eye on things during his absence. He sincerely hoped that not all the horses would be dead from hunger, thirst or the predators before he got back to the Circle H.

Crazy Horse stared unblinkingly into the dying miner's eyes.

'Deny Custer,' he said in a flat dead tone.

The man did as ordered.

'Now deny your evil government and your criminal country.'

'Yes . . . yes, as God is my judge, I deny them all.'

This gave the broad-faced Sioux chieftain an idea. 'Deny your God.'

'Yes, yes, I do so deny!' On the last word, the miner's voice rose to a scream which echoed shrilly around the walls of this Black Hills basin. The man was suspended upside down with his head mere inches above the Indian fire which was slowly boiling his brains. He howled when his hair finally caught fire and continued to writhe and jerk spasmodically as his clothing also caught alight. The Sioux chieftain, seated cross-legged nearby smoking a long pipe, watched expressionlessly until the final convulsion shook the frame of a man who had gone to face the Maker whom he had just denied.

Crazy Horse rose and stretched his lean body. If the brutal business just completed had lifted his dark spirits any, it did not show. Not on the broad bronzed face nor in the language of his horseman's body.

He walked up out of the basin to the knoll where his warriors were gathered. Standing motionless, he surveyed the hilly terrain granted the tribes under government decree, land which was now being invaded in increasing numbers by the swarms of illegal miners while the governments, the authorities and the US Army looked the other way.

It was all Custer's doing. He'd let them in. The Boy General continued to espouse red-white harmony whilst the miners raped the Black Hills and Custer himself sanctioned raid after raid upon the people out on the Great Plains.

Custer would die.

All would die.

But this could not happen until the Sioux had the weapons that would make it possible.

'We go,' he announced suddenly, striding to his horse. 'We meet Cunningham's man at Council Creek.'

Dabney rarely drank before midday. Today was an exception. He'd downed a double with his mid-morning coffee and was seated behind his desk with a tumbler filled with whiskey when Cole and Petrie appeared in response to his summons.

Naturally the operatives, whom Halliday had dubbed the Neat Twins, had not taken a drink. They never did, before sundown. They did everything by the book, and Dabney was responsible for the book.

Looking the pair over, Dabney was once again complimenting himself on the highly professional job he had made of setting up his subversive organization agency in the turbulent post-war years.

His purpose all along was to create an operation dealing with military and civil intelligence while dabbling in other less acceptable areas covertly. In the process he had eventually won the respect and patronage of the various governmental agencies and instrumentalities which proved to be both highly profitable to him personally while helping afford excellent cover for his many other illicit areas of endeavour.

His personnel were young, highly-trained, disciplined and quite ruthless. They had to be that way, for many of Bureau's activities demanded that its people set aside such things as patriotism and honesty and be ever ready to follow orders, no matter how unlawful, providing they came from himself.

Dabney was involved in major affairs involving large sums of money at that very moment, knowledge of which, should it fall into the wrong hands, would bring him to disgrace, ruin and most probably the hangman's noose, virtually overnight.

They were risks he accepted in the holy name of ambition.

The discovery of gold in the Black Hills of Dakota had triggered off the first trickle of illicit mining activity in the supposedly closed regions. But it was Dabney and a handful like him who'd seen the opportunity in its fullest perspective, brushed aside any consideration for the treaties or the Indians and had thrown all his organization's resources into exploiting the situation to the maximum.

His accidental uncovering of Cunningham and his organization, also surreptitiously involved in the turmoil that was the Black Hills, had been an unexpected glitch and a potential threat which Dabney had moved swiftly and decisively to eradicate.

He was pleased with progress, and yet the silent sober faces of Petrie and Cole when the pair reported back to him, warned him that he might be wise to down that shot of bourbon.

He did so and stared at them. 'Well?'

'Not a sign, we regret, Colonel,' fair Cole said

respectfully. 'We've had men patrolling the southern sections of the badlands and maintaining contact with our people at Pine Ridge and Martin, but there hasn't been a sign of Halliday since he went in.'

'It was by its very nature, a quick job, sir,' weighed in a sober Petrie, shoulders squared, hands locked behind. 'We estimate twenty-four hours would be the maximum time it would take Halliday to get in, kill Cunningham and get out again. It's been much longer than that, so we can assume—'

'I know what to assume, thank you, sir,' Dabney interrupted. He was silent for a long moment. There was much to consider. Had the Bureau's involvement in the Black Hills been less than total at the present moment, the colonel believed he would have pressed on with his full badlands campaign as planned until the fanatically dangerous Cunningham was in the ground and no longer posing any threat either to himself personally or in the Dakotas.

But the Bureau had commitments and responsibilities in the Black Hills which recent violent events had made critical. Diverting to Cunningham right now might see the Black Hills operation come unravelled, and no single man was worth that risk.

The colonel felt steady and very much in command as he issued orders. None was related to Buck Halliday. In Dabney's mind, Halliday was already dead, a victim of the war. *C'est la guerre.*

CHAPTER 5

KILLER IN A CAGE

The cigar was excellent, Halliday was forced to concede.

Of course a man like Cunningham was unlikely to have anything but the best, he mused. The man had the best hideaway from a world which shied away from cripples; the best reasons to hate just about everyone for real or imagined causes; best killers on his payroll, judging by what he'd seen.

And the best-looking Chinese wife?

He frowned over his corona where he sat at the barred window of his cell overlooking the spacious yards.

How had Lu Nin slipped so easily into his thoughts? Maybe it was because it was coming on midday, and as she'd brought his breakfast he wondered if she mightn't fetch lunch as well.

He half grinned.

He knew he was a suspicious man by nature. He

suspected almost everyone of deviousness and was seldom proven wrong.

The major, for instance. Cunningham was taking time out on a daily basis to visit and try to turn him against Dabney, as though this was some kind of moral imperative. Cunningham was good, Dabney bad. That was the message this ex-officer seemed hell-bent on hammering into fellow ex-officer Buck Halliday before he either set him loose again or killed him.

So, he figured cynically, if Cunningham believed he wasn't making sufficient progress in his brain-washing exercise, what would be smarter or more natural than to have his attractive and much younger wife stop by every now and again also to help reshape his prisoner's thinking and loyalties?

They had to get up pretty early to get the jump on Buck Halliday, he reassured himself. Yet the cliché sounded hollow to his own ears. Pumping up his vanity was unlikely to succeed right now. He might be alive – he might even get to stay that way, with a lot of luck. But nothing could alter the fact that he'd taken on a major assignment and the task had proven too big for him.

He raised his head.

The major's mustang was acting up again.

Halliday watched the horse cutting about its yard raising one hell of a dust and snorting like it was surrounded by a bunch of timber wolves salivating for horse meat.

Scowling sentries stared down from the parapets as the mustang bucked and sunfished as though hurling imaginary riders high. He wouldn't be surprised if ugly Devil was even more unpopular than himself here at the Fort.

And, of course, he mused with a crooked grin, he had more reason than most to hate that maverick's guts.

Brought down by a dumb animal! Small wonder that assorted hardcases stopped by the window from time to time to jeer. Last night, Halliday could scarcely believe it after he'd ghosted his way in as skilfully and craftily as he'd ever done in a high-danger situation, only to find the enemy waiting for him.

Where had he slipped up?

It hadn't taken his captors long to satisfy his curiosity. The wild mustang had picked up his drifting body scent above all the other familiar smells around the Fort, and identified it as alien – and promptly everyone knew.

He wondered what a certain unwashed Mexican wrangler might make of such an animal, him being such a great horse expert and all.

Cunningham appeared from his quarters to wheel his way across to the corral fence. Immediately the mustang crossed docilely to its master and thrust its shaggy head through the rails.

'My boy,' Cunningham purred, stroking the Roman nose. 'What's the matter, hmm? Tell papa all about it.'

Halliday concentrated on the man with a pensive frown.

According to Cunningham's own account of it, during the battle of Vicksburg his company had been cut off and Dabney was sent to relieve him. Dabney decided it was a suicide mission and deliberately held back, leaving Cunningham's company to be cut to pieces. Cunningham was crippled but survived, only to face a court martial brought about by Dabney who accused him of cowardice in the face of the enemy, the very charge Cunningham intended bringing against the colonel. The court believed Dabney and Cunningham was cashiered in disgrace, mangled physically, and judging by the man's carry-on with that dumb horse now, so Halliday speculated, maybe brain-damaged as well.

There seemed little doubt that Cunningham was likely just as evil and dangerous as Dabney had painted him, that ridding the West of a man of this caliber would likely be construed as a public service.

Yet despite this, and the fact that Cunningham would most likely kill him, Halliday knew that deep down he was actually relieved that he'd failed in his assignment.

Certainly, he'd been prepared to kill when he came here. It had seemed he had no choice – yesterday. But despite the fact that he'd killed his share and maybe more in his time, he refused to believe that made him any kind of killer, just a man who undertook dangerous ventures and was ready to protect himself at all times.

He smelt chop suey.

Lu Nin appeared outside. She was holding a covered tray as she paused to speak with Sergei. They appeared to be arguing. The woman called out to her husband at the corral. Cunningham gestured, indicating she was to be admitted to the cell. Sergei unlocked the brig door with a scowl, and soon Halliday found himself tieing into the chop suey and doing his level best to keep his eyes off his captor's lovely wife.

He had nothing against beautiful faces and lithe bodies, indeed there couldn't be many who were more for them. But the ever-present possibility of death somehow made him even more acutely aware of all the wonderful and desirable things he would miss out on if he were to die here – and lithe bodies had to be way up there near the top of the list.

But he wanted to live, get away, maybe even get square with his enemies whoever they turned out to be. He did not want to be diverted by black-lashed eyes, that old familiar feeling, or a lilting voice which tinkled like branch water rippling over sun warmed stones, right now.

But he was.

She was a handsome woman by any yardstick. And anything but a happy one, judging by certain signs he detected as she moved about the cell.

He glanced out. Cunningham had gone back inside while Sergei sat smoking in the shade, occasionally flexing his muscles. Halliday again waved through the bars and the great bulk stirred angrily, glaring balefully back and fingering the machete hanging from his six-inch belt.

It had been instant antagonism between the prisoner and the hardest man in the badlands. Cunningham's powerhouse saw himself as numero uno here, and Halliday with his reputation and arrogance was regarded as an instant challenge. In response, Halliday barely spared the man a second thought. He was largely focused on the question of just how much time he might have left.

There was even more activity across at the storehouses and stables today than yesterday. Sweating men were loading crates into small, sturdy wagons that looked designed to handle the difficult badlands terrain. He sighted several Chinese and Sioux amongst the others. All wore sidearms and looked like fighters.

Cunningham was an Indian sympathizer. He'd learned that much during their talks. But was he also a gunrunner? Someone was shipping weapons into the Black Hills tribes and Halliday's suspicions of his captor were deepening by the day.

Not that it mattered over much if his suspicions should prove correct or otherwise though, he mused cynically. Not now. The wartime Halliday had been patriotic enough, but patriotism played little part in the hanging-by-the-fingernails existence of this big man mopping up the last of Lu Nin's excellent chop suey. Even right or wrong seemed pretty irrelevant right now. All he wanted to do was to stay alive. All else was just moonshine and buffalo dust.

As he cleaned up the last of the juices he was grunting monosyllabic responses to the woman's many questions about himself, the outside world – his love life.

His love life?

He stopped eating to stare. Had he heard right? She smiled, dark eyes shining.

'At last I have caught your attention, Buckley. You were miles away.'

He leaned back to pick his teeth.

'So, you don't really want to know if I'm married or not, then?'

'That is your affair.' She turned serious. 'Are you not afraid, Buckley? I am afraid for you.'

'You reckon he'll kill me?'

'He likes you and sincerely wishes to convince you about the colonel. But even I cannot be certain he will not have you shot.'

'Well, I can't gripe, can I? I mean, given half a chance, I'd have blasted your husband and been back in Wichita gettin' patted on the back by now. I'd kill any jasper who tried to kill me. Cunningham's likely cut from the same cloth. I'll hate him if he does it, but at least I'd understand why.'

Lu Nin rose and moved to the windows. She had married Cunningham before he made his decision to relocate in the badlands, she had informed Halliday. This was before he began to deteriorate, she'd added. He had encouraged her to bring in several family members and friends, who had taken quickly to the adventurous, independent life style offering at the Fort. Lu Nin had hinted that Cunningham had over time grown obsessive about the Black Hills situation involving his friends, the Sioux. But it was not until Dabney invaded the badlands to uncover Cunningham's set-up that his real deterioration had begun.

She touched on this now. She refused to confirm or deny that the major was gun-running to the Sioux but was emphatic that his chance contact with Dabney had whipped up all his old bitterness and hatred against the man. She feared that his commitment to destroying the man who had virtually destroyed him would consume him and perhaps bring them all to ruin.

'So?' He was phlegmatic. If he was focused on anything, it was escape. Two things. Escape, and Lu Nin's exquisite beauty.

She turned and caught the look in his eye.

'I want to get away, Buckley. I think he knows it, and so has me closely watched. I don't wish to die out here, or be brought to trial somewhere if he's caught for whatever it is he's doing.'

Halliday was eager to follow up this line of conversation, but at that moment a key grated in the lock and Abilene entered the cell, slender and erect in dark shirt and Levis and looking cold about the eyes.

'The major's waiting to eat with you, Ma'am.'

She left.

Halliday blew a smoke ring at the gunman.

'What are you cooking up, Halliday?'

'Can't you smell the chop suey?'

Abilene jerked his sleek head. 'You and her. What in hell is going on?'

Halliday rose, stretching himself to full height. Abilene stood five eight, tops.

'Me and Lu Nin? Why, we're in love and are plannin' a spring weddin', of course. You could be the best man, only I doubt that you are.'

The gunman fingered his sixgun handle.

'Some way or other, you've got the major bamboozled, Halliday. He sees you as an officer and a gentlemen from his old outfit, and it's important to him that you believe his version of what happened. I be damned if he doesn't think you're something special, even if in truth you're just another two-bit backshooter not good enough to carry grits to a raccoon.'

He held up a silencing hand as Halliday made to retort.

'No, don't bother trying to explain one damn thing. I don't want to know. I just want you to know that even if you've got him and maybe her thinking confused, I know what you are. I'm watching you every minute, and the first half-smart move you make you'll be dead as dog meat.'

'I don't reckon the major would like that, somehow. He wants me alive, runt.'

'Why would he?'

'Use your brain, if you run to one. I'm Dabney's man, and the major wants Dabney's guts for gaiters. Startin' to get it? I'll spell it out. I'd make a first-rate hostage if Cunningham wanted to get an edge on Dabney, and he wants that worse than anythin'.'

'That Chinese bitch. She told you that?'

Halliday smiled crookedly.

Hunting a credible reason to explain why he was still alive, he'd just fired his best shot in the dark and it appeared to have hit home. Cunningham saw him as a hostage in the territory-sized poker game he was playing with the man he hated. He knew that now.

Realizing he'd been tricked, Abilene whipped out his gun and smashed it across his face. Halliday saw double and spat blood, but didn't react. Abilene's narrow face burned as he let himself out. Mocking laughter followed him.

'*Por favor, señor*, but have you seen this *hombre?*'

The rugged citizen of Wichita was in every way a typical citizen who extolled America as the land of the free yet hated the Irish, the Swedes, the Germans and the Dutch – but particularly the Mexicans – reared back from the runt under the floppy black sombrero, then curiously squinted at the grainy photograph being held up before his eyes.

'Who is he?' he wanted to know.

'My *amigo*, Señor Halliday.'

'He's your buddy?' this equality-loving American snorted, stamping off. 'In that case I wouldn't wanna know him even if I had seen him, which I ain't.'

Teo Caraso sighed. He lowered his rump to the curb and swabbed his brow. A freighter laden with buffalo hides rumbled by raising enough dust to choke a black dog. He figured he'd covered roughly two-thirds of the streets and all he'd gathered were insults and indifference. Maybe he would be better off back under his bridge by the Republican at Topeka.

He sighed. He shook his head.

That was quitting talk, he knew. He must not give up so easily.

The very next street he entered was named Federal. It looked no more promising than the others, yet the third man to whom he showed his photograph scratched his thatch, closed one eye,

70

then snapped his fingers.

'Sure, I seen him, *amigo*. Big geezer ridin' a blocky dun and sort of actin' like he thought he was . . . you know . . . somethin' special. That sound like him?'

'That is Señor Halliday. He was here, *señor*?'

The man drew him further out into the street to point out a collection of buildings set back from the road.

'I seen him there four or five days back, buddy. But I wouldn't go sniffin' around there if I was you.'

'Why not, *compadre*?'

'On account it's weird is why, sonny. I mean strange.'

Caraso smiled wearily. 'Señor, my whole life is mucho weird. I even have weird *amigos*, such as Señor Halliday and . . .'

He broke off. The man was walking away. He had that effect on people. It could be to do with his body odor. Teo Caraso did not bathe. Neither did he take offence at the reaction of men who hated Mexicans.

He set off along Federal.

It was shock for those on watch at the Bureau to see a ragged Mexican sporting a floppy black sombrero and leading a block-headed mule, calmly stroll into the wagon yard so nonchalantly and unconcerned. A dozen guns covered him before he could drag off his hat, flash a gap-toothed grin and say, ' 'Allo, *amigos*.'

That was how Halliday's sometime sidekick wound up in a room without windows surrounded by several cold-eyed young men, with a thin trickle of blood running from his left nostril, a dazed expression on his homely pan and a certain degree of apprehension.

'*Que?*' he panted, staring from face to face. Their fists and guns didn't scare him as much as their clean-shaven faces and sober clothing. Caraso mistrusted the clean and well-dressed. At times Halliday bordered on that category, but as the Mexican only trusted him about ten percent of the time that was no big problem. 'What did I do?'

'We ask the questions here, killer,' Clanton Cole snarled in his face, and proceeded to do just that. They interrogated him until realizing he was looking for Halliday, that he claimed to be his friend, and that he was indeed toting a grubby photograph of his missing *compañero* around inside his hat.

This development got him into see Dabney, who had to ask for someone to fetch a bottle of scent before he could concentrate sufficiently to demand the prisoner reveal exactly what the hell he was doing here.

Caraso obliged. He might not smell too flash but he could be articulate and convincing when circumstances demanded. He was Halliday's partner and he was developing an uneasy feeling that all was not well with him. Could Señor Dabney throw some light on where he might be located?

Dabney withdrew out of earshot to confer with his staff. One clung to the notion that he could still be some kind of plant, possibly of Cunningham's, and that they should 'disappear' him, just to be on the safe side. But another had dug deeper into their background material on Halliday to confirm the fact that he was indeed at times observed traveling in the company of one Caraso, described in intelligence documents as 'an unemployed horse thief and guitar player'.

Satisfied at last, Dabney finally admitted that Halliday was indeed employed by him on a highly important mission, from which he was long overdue.

To their surprise, Caraso grinned to hear this.

'The *señoritas*,' he said wisely. 'Always the *señoritas*. He—'

'He went into the South Dakota badlands to hunt an evil man and he's four days overdue,' Dabney interrupted sharply. 'Still think he's screwing around?'

Eventually Caraso found himself back out on Federal Street with Joachim, in the background, three wooden-faced gunmen standing in line watching to make sure he left: when they found he could throw no further light on Halliday's situation and thus was of no use to the Bureau.

A thoughtful Teo sought out Wichita's sole Mexican eatery where he over-indulged in tortillas and frijoles and two huge bowls of chili con carne. Topping this off with a slab of pie and three cups of powerful coffee, he staggered off belching into the night, physically in poor shape but mentally crystal clear now.

Halliday needed him.

The big man would rather die the death of a thousand stilettos than ever admit he needed help, but it was true that there had been occasions in the past when Caraso had hauled his irons out of the fire and and saved his bacon.

It was almost midnight before Wichita's night-watch sighted a grubby Mexican astride a dusty mule crossing the train tracks and heading in the direction of the north trail.

Teo Caraso was badlands bound. He was concerned about Halliday's whereabouts. He still believed it all had something to do with women.

CHAPTER 6

HIGHTAILIN' TIME

Drenched in the orange moonlight peculiar to the badlands the strange construction might have almost passed for a huge hacienda, possibly occupied by a town mayor or the local rail or cattle baron. But broad daylight always highlighted the grim reality of the Fort, and on this night at least, with a gentle breeze blowing across the serried, broken country and that high moon rising, with somewhere the faint sounds of a nighthawk's harmonica serenading the stars, Cunningham's stronghold was an almost romantic place to be. With extra scouting squads out in the badlands to keep watch in the event Dabney should dispatch forces searching for Halliday, the night guard was light tonight. Three men paced the parapets and another two walked their silent beats down in the quadrangle.

The yard guards were both Chinese who maintained a discreet distance from the brig where something was going on that was none of their damn business. Lu Nin had made it pretty plain upon her stealthy arrival at his cell that she was prepared to do anything, give him anything he wanted, if that was his price for throwing in his lot with her.

Halliday had been tempted; he was more easily tempted than most. But romance, or whatever passed for it in this alien place in the heart of the grotesque badlands, was the farthest thing from his mind. A woman back in Arkansas had helped him try and forget a girl with blue eyes without success. Clara was still with him even if they were through. His only interest in the lovely Chinese was whether she represented a chance to escape. He hoped.

He sat listening to her soft words in his cell, her silken black hair a dark cloud in his face as she passed him yet another cup of sweet Chinese tea.

Lu Nin had arranged the Chinese guards whom she could trust, had secured the cell key and made her needs only too clear to the prisoner the moment they were alone.

She wished to escape the Fort and her husband.

Halliday, with his love of both danger and beautiful women, full knew the risk he was taking in her being here with him like this. At this stage of his imprisonment he seemed to be making strong progress with the complex Cunningham, who seemed to admire his bravery and with whom he shared a strong sympathy for the Sioux, whose lands were being invaded in the Black Hills, and who were perishing in numbers because of this.

He had every good reason to follow up this tenuous rapport he seemed to have developed with his captor – but surely should Cunningham discover his wife was visiting him by night and talking treachery of some kind, he might be slaughtered on the spot. It was a huge risk, but he was a risk-taker by nature. Besides, he might be misreading his rapport with Cunningham. For all he knew the man might be calmly and coldly planning to have him extermi- nated right at that very moment.

'It would be possible, Buckley,' she was saying – he loved the lilt she put on his name. 'I have some six or seven men I can count on here . . . there are vehicles, and I know the route to Osage. I have been tempted to flee many times before, but I was always aware that to succeed I would need more help than my fellow countrymen.'

She shuddered.

'Sergei can track anything anywhere, man or beast. And you can see what a fierce brute he is. . . .' She leaned forward. 'But you are a warrior, a samurai. With you, with my loyal ones and with just a little good fortune we—'

'Could get ourselves killed?'

He liked the idea, was prepared to take almost any desperate chance. But horse sense warned that to make a run burdened by a female and some gentle Chinese servants would be a recipe for disaster. True, he could let her assist him escape, then dump them and strike out alone. But he had enough on his conscience already without that one.

The woman rose and came round to stand behind his chair. Her hands were gentle on his neck.

'My husband will kill you, Buckley,' she said, her tone low and intense. 'He is a wonderful man twisted and ruined by life. You will surely die if you send me away. Please?'

Her words flowed over him. She murmured against his ear and Halliday looked past her dark head at that fat old moon. And for the moment the soldier, rancher, wagon boss and now potential assassin just let it take him along for the ride for the time being . . . he just soaked it up. . . .

Movement caught his eye. Someone was crossing the quadrangle. He rose and stepped quickly and silently to the bars. It was Sergei. In the silent heart of the night the hulking giant was walking without a breath of sound, tobacco smoke trailing over his shoulder. The great animal head turned and for a moment Halliday caught the feral gleam of dark eyes seeming to probe directly at him, though he stood in darkness.

The man vanished and Halliday found his resolve weakening. Was it not possible that 'die one way or die another' were his only alternatives?

He sighed. 'Tell me some more about how, with who . . . and just how well you know this trail out to Osage, honey.'

Her eyes filled with tears of relief and she began talking again, the words tripping over one another.

From his chair, he gazed up at her admiringly as he reached for one of the cigars Cunningham had provided him. She was truly beautiful, he mused. And he'd always had a theory that beautiful women deserved to get what they wanted, simply because of being beautiful.

'. . . I have a pistol, I believe I could get more. And bullets, we may need bullets . . .'

'Guess we may,' he murmured ironically, searching for his vestas. 'What kind of pistol?'

'A thirty-eight.'

He nodded. A pop gun. He scraped a vesta into life and applied it to the tip of the cigar, sucked it into fragrant life. 'Go on, beautiful. I can tell you honestly your plan's a guarantee I won't nod off.'

'I have already made arrangements to escape tomorrow night should you agree to take this terrible chance. My guard friends will assist us and ensure the other guards do not see us. They will pretend to shoot at us but they will miss.' She went to her things and he heard the soft chink of metal as she produced a set of keys. 'These unlock the pumphouse gate. All we need are horses and a little luck if the turret guards open fire.'

He sat staring up at her. He couldn't figure if he wanted to help her or himself. Her 'plan' might be a winner or it might be suicide. His brain appeared to have slowed its function. He felt he was surrendering logic and clutching at desperation.

'Let me see your gun, honey.'

Wordlessly, she took the pearl-handled .38 Special from her pocketbook and placed it in his palm. He studied it with a detached expression. Cunningham's bunch seemed to have enough heavy weapons to take on Custer's cavalry and he had a little .38! But gazing at the window and that slice of precious sky, he knew he'd already decided. He knew he would attempt it despite the strident voice in the back of his mind nagging about the uncertainty, the terrain, the handicap of other people slowing them. The odds here were way too long. But what was the option?

'Life,' he grunted, feeling a chill grip his guts as he rose to move to the window. 'Why does a man gripe about it? He knows what it is from the outset, doesn't he?'

'What is it?' She had no idea what he was talking about, what he was thinking.

'It's just a whole bunch of ten-to-one against, is what.'

'Is that bad?'

'It's the way things are.' He went to the window. 'Looks OK for you to go.' He winked. 'OK. See you later if the cricks don't rise.'

She smiled and touched his cheek.

'You are the strange one, so fierce yet so funny.'

'That's me right enough, laugh-a-minute Halliday. Now skeedaddle before someone sees you and starts in trying to figure what you were doing here, little lady.'

Lu Nin left. Halliday stared at the badlands moon. How did a man get into such fixes? Next time somebody claimed his marker on a debt of honour, he reckoned he would say, 'Thanks, but no thanks.'

He shook his head and smiled grimly.

Who was he trying to kid? A man was who he was, all the bad and just a little bit of good. But should he survive Mrs Cunningham's hair-raising escape plan, he was crystal clear on what his course would be. He would not go through with the killing, no matter what. He'd have to figure some way to convince Dabney that the task he'd assigned him to do was both impossible and unjust. He'd always remain in Dabney's debt, but the man was asking too much of him. The colonel must simply figure out another way to eliminate Cunningham. Dabney struck him as eminently resourceful, the kind of man who'd know a hundred ways to kill somebody.

He stared across the compound at the Cunninghams' quarters. The light in the study where the major heaved his wasted body about on his bars while plotting whatever it was that kept him solvent and occupied out here, still burned brightly in the late night.

His jaw muscles worked.

Cunningham was a crazy. Had to be. He was obsessed with Dabney, hated the Army for what he believed it had done to him, was certainly involved in illicit gun-running to the Indians on a major scale while paradoxically happy to occupy the high moral ground on ethical issues as though he was one of the few remaining men of honor left in the West.

And yet he still almost liked the man – even if he was planning a bust-out tomorrow night in which he knew he would be prepared to slaughter every man-jack here, including Cunningham himself, if that was what it took.

How come?

It wasn't hard to figure. Dabney had been an admirable fighting man and commanding officer as well as the man who'd saved his life, yet now he saw him as a man of straw.

On the other hand, the crippled, obsessive Cunningham had something rare. He didn't doubt the man was a crook and most likely a killer to boot. Yet he was nothing like Dabney, nowhere near as ruthless and predictable.

Halliday had come here specifically to kill Cunningham. He should be dead by now by rights, yet his life had been spared thus far apparently because the major appeared to regard him both as an ex-soldier and a man of honor. He sensed now that, in an almost touching way, crippled Cunningham desperately wanted to convince at least one former 25th Cavalry warrior of his innocence in that incident on the battlefields so long ago which had destroyed his reputation. He sighed and shook his head. Then again, maybe he simply liked the man because he was obviously a little crazy. Loyal Teo Caraso believed Halliday himself was a little loco, so maybe it was just a case of like attracting like.

The longer he stood watching the moon and thinking on what he planned to attempt the next night, the more he was inclined to think that flea-bitten wetback might have him figured just about right.

How could a day be forty-eight hours long?

Yet night eventually came to the badlands, the Fort and the prison cell and Halliday was as ready as he would ever be. Doubts had plagued throughout the burning day. But now with lamps glowing softly and a lonesome nighthawk serenading the sprinkled stars, he felt relaxed, like a prize fighter in his corner waiting for the bell. He'd shaved, eaten sparingly, exchanged the occasional insults with Sergei and Abilene who watched him like buzzards. He had a hunch that by the time he'd finished this splendid example of the Cuban cigar-maker's art in his hand, it would be time. Time to pack his .38, sharpen himself up and get ready. He'd never felt readier.

It was a Halliday habit at times like this to put himself through a confidence-boosting ritual; the greater the risk the more confidence he needed. And this night was promising to be about as high risk as a situation could get. He reminded himself of the scrapes he'd survived, the badmen he'd beaten with the guns, the way Lady Luck seemed to favor him when the chips were really down, as was the case right now.

Soon a combination of will-power, self-assurance and a gunfighter's pride had lifted his spirits and honed his nerves razor sharp. Gazing out he was convinced in his own mind now that all he could see out there were, not hardcases or danger men, but rather tenth-raters and losers of three different races who were prepared to live out here like meek little prairie dogs under Cunningham's thumb simply because they couldn't make it in the real world.

He'd cut his teeth on little people like this and had graduated to the big league before he turned twenty.

This would be child's play!

And it was a barely audible voice that whispered, 'You hope, *amigo*.'

The whisper faded as a key grated in the lock. He had not heard her come. That was a good sign. She wouldn't let him down. They would make it together. They almost did.

Standing in the velvety shadows outside with the .38 solid and reassuring in his belt and a calm Lu Nin at his side, Halliday swept the compound with eyes that missed nothing. The yard guards were out of sight, just as she'd promised. Cunningham's wild mustang was acting up and snorting around its corral but nobody seemed to be paying it any attention. A noisy gambling game was taking place in the men's quarters, slow-moving figures walked the parapets and the dim outlines of horses were visible in the barn yard down by the pumphouse gate.

He gave her a quick admiring look. She'd set it all up like a pro. All he had to do was prove he was one as well.

Clinging to the shadows, the couple hurried around the brig corner then followed the narrow alleyway running between that building and the wagon shed. They ducked and froze as a familiar silhouette appeared in the lighted doorway of the mud brick quarters which housed Cunningham's elite, including Sergei and Abilene.

The herculean silhouette was Sergei. Halliday fingered his .38. After what seemed a long time, the huge man went back inside and closed the door.

The next half-minute saw them reach the barn yard without incident. There were saddles and harness concealed behind a water trough. Halliday was readying the mounts for the trail while the woman slipped down to the gate with a soft jingle of keys.

The gate creaked open and unexpectedly the head and shoulders of a sentry immediately appeared over the parapet thirty feet above, peering down. 'Who goes? That you, Abilene?'

Halliday froze. Trouble was, Lu Nin didn't. She began to run back towards him. The sentry sighted her dim shape, saw the open gate, instantly pumped a bullet into the sky.

'Hold up!' he shouted. Then, 'Trouble at the pump gate!'

Halliday watched what happened next with a kind of frozen horror. Still thirty yards distant, Lu Nin stumbled and fell. The sentry challenged again. She didn't respond. He threw his rifle to his shoulder and fired. The woman screamed and rolled out of the patch of moonlight. In alarm and confusion she sprang to her feet and ran blindly away from Halliday's position, panicking as the entire Fort erupted into a bedlam of sound with running figures rushing every which way and horses rearing wildly in their stalls.

He had a shaved second to assess the situation. The whole plan was blown away. It couldn't be salvaged. Nothing could be salvaged, unless . . .

The half-opened gate was drawing him. He knew he could well die should he make a try for it. But how long would he last once they knew he'd tried to bust out anyway? His head swam as the clamor and turmoil increased. The gate was suddenly the Liberty Bell, the siren song and the beckoning hand of destiny.

In an instant he was in the saddle and heeling

85

away down the pathway, leaning low over the horse's neck and riding hands and heels.

Now he was in the moonlight.

'It's that goddamn gunfighter! Halliday!'

The wild shout was the precursor to the bullet that struck the reaching horse in the ribs. Spinning end over end, the animal slammed into the wall by the gateway, upside down and threshing in agony.

The huge body came crashing to earth where a dazed Halliday had lain but a moment before. Exploding to his feet, he shot through the gateway like a startled antelope and zig-zagged for the river like a hunted animal aware that every stride could be its last.

They were too eager to cut him down.

Singing slugs gouged the earth all about him but Halliday was still unscathed by the time he dived headlong off the high bank and vanished beneath the surface, where he remained, swimming downstream until his lungs howled for mercy.

His head broke the surface as the main gate clanked open a hundred yards upslope. He heard barking hounds and men shouting orders, punctuated by the occasional crash of a wild shot.

But still no sign of mounted pursuit.

A shadowy fissure beckoned ahead as he hauled his big body from the water. At headlong speed he plunged into it and sped away into the moonshadows. He turned his head. He could no longer see the Fort from this position, which meant they could not see him.

The hunters failed to catch him in the first mile – or the next ten.

*

The moving dot on the face of the plains slowly grew into a blob, a centaur shape and finally evolved into a Mexican astride an ugly mule threading between the gopher holes and prairie dog villages which studded this sweep of border plain.

'Aaii, Joachim, the great good thing about riding you through this sad life, is that with your knobby backbone, your evil disposition and the gait of the armadillo, they will say, "Teo, you have done your Purgatory on earth; pass on through these golden gates and we will fetch some liniment to rub on your bottom." Do you not agree this is a good thing, oh bony one?'

The mule plodded on phlegmatically, placing one hoof ahead of the other, a dumb brute beneath a broiling sun who wanted nothing of conversation, irony, sarcasm or 'wit'.

It took a long slow time to surmount the upslope that seemed to rise forever, sorely testing man and mule. Then suddenly they topped it out and the rider jerked the reins to drag the beast to a halt.

'*Madre!*' Caraso breathed. 'I speak of heaven but surely this is hell!'

Before him lay a vast and brutal landscape, alien country that might well indeed have been shaped by Lucifer's fine hand, and the sun-stricken rider would hardly have been surprised to glimpse beyond the sinister River Styx of the Underworld with Charon the Ferryman carrying the world's lost souls to their final abode in hell.

It might look like hell but he knew it was just the Dakota badlands.

Mile upon mile it reached into the north, a nightmare labyrinth of gullies, arroyos, sudden outcroppings, sun-bleached grass and barely a trace of brush or vegetation.

And Teo Caraso thought bitterly: 'How like Amigo Halliday to come to such a place simply to make it so much difficult for his one true friend to find him. Surely, as the blessed virgin knows, if there is the sweet easy way to do something, or the big dumb hard way, every time he will choose the hard and the worst. . . .'

His voice trailed away. He realized how strange it would appear – a solitary Sonoran so far from his native land, sitting an ugly mule under a blazing sun on the fringe of this land of dragons – and talking to himself.

Slowly his eyes played over the scene before focusing upon the rearing outline of a tan-flanked mesa in the middle distance.

He fingered the battered set of field glasses slung around his scraggy neck. They were good glasses which enabled him to see great distances. But was it reasonable to expect that in all this crazy landscape he might expect them to be able to detect just one *hombre?*

He shrugged philosophically, booted Joachim in the slats and set off. It stood to reason he'd see a damn sight more from atop that high tan mesa than down here amongst the prairie dogs and gophers.

Something slithered and clattered in the brush, causing the mule to start. 'Rattlesnakes,' murmured Caraso. This wonderful gringo land had everything.

CHAPTER 7

GUNS NORTH

Dabney raised a gloved hand to bring the column to a halt. They'd railroaded deep into Nebraska but were now horsebacking along an old Texas-Montana cattle trail for the South Dakota border, the supremo of the Bureau along with upwards of thirty men with guns.

Only twice since its inception several years earlier had Dabney's covertly criminal organization quit the Wichita headquarters in this sort of strength, each time a crisis.

The colonel was not prepared to label this operation a crisis as yet. But should the situation prove sufficiently serious with the potential to deteriorate further, he would certainly take what he termed in his military way, appropriate action.

Halliday had failed to kill Cunningham. That had been a bitter pill to swallow, particularly in light of his expectations for the man he'd gone to such lengths to recruit. Cunningham in his grave would have relieved much of Dabney's concern that his life was in constant danger.

But equally as important was the Bureau's latest intelligence on the worsening situation in the Black Hills involving miners, Indians and the small Army outpost seeking to prevent open warfare from erupting around the strategically positioned Crow Creek Stockade on the Singing River.

The commander of the stockade, Harrelson, was a covert business associate of the colonel's, a ruthless huckster on the rise and as corrupt as the Bureau chief himself.

Swinging from his saddle to eat chow standing up whilst consulting with his lieutenants, Dabney appeared neither troubled nor corrupt. What he looked like out here under the big open skies in his tailored riding gear and his air of natural authority, was what he had once been, namely a distinguished leader of men.

He still led but was no longer distinguished.

Ever since the first gold-seekers had slunk into the Black Hills to begin illegal mining in the mineral-rich Indian lands two years earlier, Dabney had been heavily involved in this criminal activity through his close association with Harrelson, the corrupt army commander at Crow Creek.

Between them the partners had set up an elaborate quasi-legal system of granting high-priced mining leases to hundreds and eventually thousands of diggers who had no legal right to so much as step upon Black Hills soil, much less plunder its treasures.

Treading a wary but highly profitable path between blatant fraud and superficial support for the Sioux in their struggle against the miners, Dabney and Captain Harrelson had supported, aided and abetted the illicit mining, providing through front organizations all manner of necessary protection against the Indians. Add to that the milling and sale of the gold and the exclusive supply of provisions and mining equipment, the enterprises had paid off handsomely and had made both the captain and the former colonel wealthy men.

Neither desired peace in the Black Hills. So their joint enterprises involving the hiring and utilizing of gangs of Indian-killers who roamed the Hills almost at will, doing their bloody, stealthy works, guaranteed the region remained in constant turmoil. If the situation were ever resolved, and Washington should find the will and the funding to restore order and maintain the red-white border lines, their money river would dry up and two 'respected' military men might well end up in court or upon the gallows.

Stroking his jaw as he surveyed the intimidating landscape before him, Dabney reflected on the two prime factors that had seen him take the rare step of quitting his plush, secure headquarters in Wichita and exposing himself to the uncertainties of one of the most dangerous regions in the entire land.

The first was the ever increasing pressure to 'do something' about the perceived Cunningham threat, now that his elaborate attempt to kill the man himself had plainly ended in failure. The other was to investigate at first hand his spies' growing conviction that the Black Hills Sioux were about to receive a large shipment of rifles. Should this eventuate, it could dramatically alter the balance of power in the region, or possibly overbalance it altogether.

Having finally uncovered Cunningham's presence in the badlands, the Bureau now felt certain that the menacing increase of modern weapons in the hands of the Sioux was emanating from his enemy. It would certainly make sense for the Dabney-hating Cunningham to furnish the Sioux with modern armaments in the current tinderbox situation, thus empowering the Indians to defend their own patch and possibly even get to hurl the intruders out altogether.

Deep down, Dabney knew he'd always intended that Cunningham would have to die sooner or later if he was ever to know real dominance and peace of mind in the region.

He certainly didn't wish to be out here in the wilds preparing for what could prove a bloody showdown today. But if the outcome was the demise of his enemy then he was prepared to play the game hard and not quit until it was won, regardless of the cost.

And now that decision had been made and he was back in the outdoor-action mode that had once been so familiar, the colonel was feeling just like his old formidable self, and it showed.

'Guess I almost hate to bother you with boring details when you're looking so chipper and rested, sir,' reported Clanton Cole, clutching a colored map in both hands. 'But there's a small problem here . . .'

'That's quite all right, Cole. What is it?'

The problem concerning a decision between making directly for the stockade, or searching east of the Black Hills for the gunrunners' possible supply route, was quickly solved.

They would search for the supply route, Dabney decided emphatically.

He was hoping to uncover that route with the prospect of it leading them directly to Cunningham's badlands stronghold.

They needed to chop off the supply at its source. But it was infinitely more important to Dabney – even more important than the threat to his golden milch cow in the hills – that he make contact with and finish off Cunningham before he got the chance to finish him.

Dabney was certain Cunningham would know by now that he'd dispatched the very best man he could find to kill him. Cunningham would not take that lying down – he could not. Dabney had upped the stakes in sending Halliday after his foe. Now Cunningham must strike back before Dabney regrouped and tried again.

All Dabney's secret uncertainties and doubts were aroused again and eating at his guts. He wasn't sleeping nights and the bottle was his best friend. This impressive leader of men had been a crypto coward in the war, and the leopard hadn't changed its spots. First Cunningham, then on to Crow Creek. He made it sound simple but was nothing like sure it would pan out that way.

But a man acting out of fear and uncertainty can be every bit as dangerous as another standing on the rock of his courage. And Dabney was an excellent actor capable of concealing the fact that he secretly believed the foe might prove stronger than they feared, and that a lot of men could die before the old enmity which had been born on the bloody fields of Vicksburg was finally laid to rest.

Nonetheless, he still presented a reassuring picture of confidence as he mounted up, gave them a catch-cry they could savor, and led them on: 'Cunningham first, then on to Crow Creek!'

He rode lead and they watched him admiringly. He was a natural actor. His whole life had been based on his ability to convey the image of strength which concealed the real man beneath. He furtively ran a finger around his immaculate collar as the miles rolled beneath them. He was remembering just how many reasons crippled Cunningham had to hate him. Halliday's failed attempt to kill the man on his behalf had added just one more to that long list.

Halliday stared back.

The pursuers were out there strung along the east horizon like tiny beads on a string, their movement barely perceptible. But they were riders, he knew, manhunters with guns and dogs and an intimate knowledge of the terrain they searched.

But the badlands could be a friend or an enemy, and Halliday had made it his friend.

It had not taken him long to realize that in viciously eroded country such as this a man must stick to the bottoms of the endless myriad of gullies to avoid being seen.

Those dedicated manhunters could hunt, howl, berate the hounds for losing his scent, and make a fine intimidating display as they rode. But if they couldn't see him, how in hell could they find him?

He hunkered down to rest and nurse his unease. Despite their numbers, it was not concern about the main pursuit party to the east which he figured would be being led by Sergei and Abilene.

It was the redskin scouts that bothered him.

It was now mid-afternoon. Mid-morning and many exhausting miles back he'd seen the Fort posse split up with roughly one half continuing on together but the other half splitting off into small-swift riding parties of horsemen who'd fanned out quickly and more widely than he could hope to keep track of.

These small parties could be anywhere. Up along the next branch gully, maybe. Or hiding behind that grassy hummock yonder. There were limitless places an enemy might conceal himself in a land that might have been designed for such lethal cat and mouse games.

He shrugged, rose, jogged on.

Sure, he reassured himself. Right now they could be in this gully he was travelling, or they could be ten miles away. He would go with the latter notion for now.

Powerful legs ate up the miles. Halliday was weary but his will was fresh. The bust-out had been half-botched, yet was a small miracle the way it had panned out. Too bad she hadn't made it. He had a hunch he really cared for glossy-bodied Lu Min.

Really liked her. Or had done. Had she been hit? Might she not be dead by this? He thought she might well be if Cunningham believed she had been involved in his escape.

So it goes.

He had no presentiment of imminent danger as he rounded a sharp bend in the endless gully a long hour later. It came as a shock to jog around a grassy shoulder and come face to face with a giant of a man leading a limping and sweat-streaked quarter horse, an all too familiar giant who stopped on a dime and jerked his .44 up to firing level, his face contorted with triumphant rage.

Sergei!

Halliday stared into the muzzle of the black .44 and froze. His .38 was in his deep pocket. No chance of getting it out. He didn't want shooting anyway. That would surely draw the rest of posse. He had enough on his plate without that. More than enough most likely.

He dare not charge. That would be begging for the bullet. But he dare not do nothing. . . .

'There must be a God!' the giant gloated, black eyes raking him head to foot. 'You alive, no gun . . . me stumblin' into you takin' a short cut . . . me still alive! A miracle!'

Studying the brutish face, Halliday felt a flutter of hope. He'd never passed up an opportunity to stare this killer down, made cracks about him within his hearing, and denigrated him to whoever cared to listen. It was a technique he often employed against a perceived enemy to intimidate him and cause uncertainty and so reduce any danger the man might pose.

'Not so mouthy now, are you Halliday?' Sergei was enjoying this as he let the reins drop and drew a little close. The man radiated a murderous confidence, and why not? 'You look like a dog wolf what's been run by a relay of hounds . . . I can smell the stink of fear comin' off you like a wave. But a big man like you couldn't be scared of . . .'

He broke off and stepped back warily as Halliday suddenly went down on one knee, both hands clutching his guts. He dry retched and shook his head slowly from side to side.

'If you want to count coup on a man you'd better get on with it, lard guts . . . That fool horse threw me an hour back, busted somethin' inside . . .'

He buckled over, waiting for the bullet he was sure must come. But instead of finishing him, Sergei began circling, cursing, accusing him of lying, branding him yellow, almost frothing in an excess of rage.

Halliday felt his heart quicken with hope. The son of a bitch wanted to kill him, but not yet.

The gun barrel slammed against the top of his skull. He fell forward convincingly – and saw the outsized boot within reach.

His right arm blurred like a striking rattler and his hand closed upon the boot. Sergei roared and reared back. Halliday retained his iron grip and employed his purchase on the boot to flip himself up out of the dirt and catch the bigger man under the jaw with the top of his skull.

Sergei reeled drunkenly. Halliday kicked upwards

and caught the man's gun arm. The weapon spun from his hand. While the gun was arcing through the air he belted the reeling figure sideways with a swinging right fist to the side of the jaw.

Sergei crashed to his back but bounced up again like something made of Indian rubber. His reflexes were lightning, and now he had a knife in his hand as he bellowed like a wounded bull. He charged.

With blood streaming from an arm slash, Halliday side-stepped, ducked and weaved. The giant was panther quick and seemingly impervious to his hardest punches. He changed tactics, backing up and feigning fear. Sergei fell for it. He threw caution to the winds and charged wildly, swinging the wicked blade in murderous arcs before him.

Halliday suddenly sidestepped, stuck out a tripping leg and the man was down. Instantly he began kicking. He kicked to the head, the neck, the chest. Sergei howled and groaned in agony but he wouldn't let him up. He must have gone a little loco for a moment. A combination of pain and exhaustion along with maybe a dozen other factors had all caught up with him in that mad moment, so much so that he was forgetting his gun.

Then he remembered and grabbed for it in his pocket. But the foresight snagged on the lining which gave the giant the split second he needed to recover his feet and rush him.

The gun finally jerked free, but not fast enough. A swinging arm as thick as a man's thigh knocked the piece from his hand, sending it flying. Another swing saw him take a stunning blow to the side of the head and be driven groggily backwards.

Sergei was every bit the fighter he professed to be!

Halliday was cursing his reckless temper now as he found himself forced to cover up and absorb a rain of crunching blows on elbows and forehands. He could have finished him when he had the chance – he should have . . .

Whack!

A fist like iron broke through his guard and caught him on the forehead. It hurt like hell and had a secondary effect. It made him realize that Buck Halliday, the rough-houser and sometime Indian fighter, who'd always believed he had the measure of any man in hand to hand combat, had just met his equal.

He was damned if he had!

Desperation and challenged vanity cleared his brain. He exploded into violent action.

Halliday ripped a pistoning right into the bigger man's guts, causing his mouth to fly open, gasping for air. The knife spilled from his hand from the shock, clattering away on stone as he jack-knifed forward.

Halliday swung a right that missed and a left that didn't. The blow landed on the back of the doubled-up Sergei's neck. He seized a handful of lank hair and rammed that big head down and smashed him in the face with his upswinging left knee.

The trick had won more than one bar-room brawl for him. It was designed to smash your opponent's nose and blind him with tears, rendering him momentarily helpless. But something went wrong, the giant's mouth was wide open and his big bone-crunching teeth sank into Halliday's knee, sank in deep and bloodily, temporarily paralyzing his lower leg.

He gasped in pain and lost balance. The gunman jerked erect, wild-eyed and dripping blood. In that split second Halliday realized again he'd met his match. In the next, as he somehow averted a panther rush and whistling fist the size of a cantaloupe, he remembered his gun.

He broke away and stumbled for the weapon. Sergei saw what he was doing and realized he couldn't stop him in time. His own weapon glinted in the sand. Huge legs pistoned him forward and he was hurling his massive body for the .44 when Halliday swept up his gun, rolled like a circus trick shooter and shot him just above the right ear. Sergei shuddered violently then went still. He didn't move again.

Halliday's breath was rasping in tortured lungs as he staggered off in search of the dead man's horse.

Eventually he crawled up the grass wall of a gully to reconnoiter, and immediately threw himself belly flat again.

With good reason.

His pain-distorted vision focused on the wavering figures of a man leading a mule coming directly his way his way from the southwest about one hundred yards distant. Gazing upwards, he realized the fight to the death had raised a visible cloud of yellow dust. At a distant sound he swivelled his head to glimpse far-off riders storming his way, attracted by the dust and the sound of the shot.

' 'Allo, *amigo!*'

Unreality gripped him like a vice. He stared, clenched his eyes shut, stared again. Through the slowly clearing film of tears and dust blurring his vision, he made out the all too familiar face of the man he'd left in charge of his horse ranch one hundred miles away.

Halliday's heart was barely in it when they holed up together in a crater-shaped hole with bullets whistling all about them like lethal hailstones.

His gun was now empty; naturally the Mexican had misplaced his weapon somewhere along the trail. Halliday almost wished Sergei had finished him off now.

It didn't take Abilene and his party long to realize they had him at their mercy. Halliday was too disgusted even to curse as they swarmed over them, howling and hooting like they'd just won the Battle of Gettysburg or something.

'Hey, *amigo*, you want some chili?'

Silence.

'Is very nice.' Slurping sounds filled the spacious, iron-barred room they called the brig. 'Ahh, this reminds this caballero of the swell good chili my sister makes when I visit on her birthday. Not my sister Angelica. She is the one who makes the fine bedspreads from Apache scalps and has the magnificent tattoo of Emperor Maximilian on her—'

'Want to die?'

'*Compañero*, why is is that you are so angry? Did I not travel one hundred miles astride that accursed mule just to search for you? Was I not ready, after seeing you hiding in the gullies like the gopher from my high place atop the mesa in a manner in which the evil ones could not, to come riding to your rescue like Don Quixote and–'

'And led the sons of bitches directly to me like I'd built a goddamn bonfire!'

'I did not know they would be this smart.'

'They're goin' to kill us. You know that don't you? The only reason they didn't do me out in the badlands was on account they figured Cunningham would want the pleasure himself. They're goin' to kill me because I came here to kill him, and they'll kill you because you're with me.'

Caraso looked woebegone. Then he brightened as he gazed through the barred window. 'Amazing! This I do not believe! Come see, *amigo.*'

Halliday remained seated on his bunk, back to the window. He could not be persuaded to look at anything. He had no interest in anything with the possible exception of Mexicide. He was as low as Death Valley's deepest well. The only brightness in the blackest hour of his life was that Lu Nin was still alive, not even hurt. Sure, he was intensely grateful for that one. But facing certain death in the company of a bad smelling and garrulous Mex almost over-weighed his relief.

'Joachim has made the friend.'

'That mule doesn't have a friend in the world. Even you hate him.'

'This is true. But the mustang with the red eye likes him, and I think Joachim likes him also.'

103

Halliday still refused to look. Yet outside in the yards, a strange happening was taking place as the mule sniffed amiably through the rails of Devil's corral, and that untamed stump tail, which was as ferociously aggressive to all other four-leggers as it was to all mankind, with the exception of Cunningham himself, stood calmly with its mane hanging in its eyes, making little grunting noises that sounded like pleasure.

Buck Halliday could not care less if the sky should fall and the dead rise wailing from their tombs. He was going to die and there was nothing he could do about it. He'd used up all his luck and options.

Or had he?

This query was posited when four armed men came and escorted him across the compound in manacles for an audience with the colonel.

On entering that strange room with the web of hand bars, he glimpsed a pale-faced Lu Nin in a doorway. He raised his eyebrows and she nodded. She was all right. He could only guess they didn't realize she had been with him, or else Cunningham was playing the forgiving husband.

Did he care one way or another?

Maybe he did.

Maybe.

The colonel kept him waiting half an hour, during which time Halliday saw several heavily laden wagons rolling out through the main gate flanked by armed riders.

The dust clouds climbing above the parapets told him the wagons were rolling southwest – towards the Black Hills.

If he weren't facing certain death he might make something of that.

As he'd done before, Cunningham rolled into the room in his wheelchair, then heaved himself out and took to his bars.

His big-shouldered prisoner eyed the man stonily yet his look was not returned. If Cunningham was in murderous mood, he was good at concealing it.

'Do you see those critters?' was his opening remark, grunting and straining his way to a window. 'I swear I'd almost given up on Devil ever making a friend – he hates the entire universe. But your friend's mule seems to have won him over.'

'No friend of mine.'

'He tried to save your life, didn't he, Buck?'

'Look, let's say we cut the crap, Cunningham. I busted out, I beefed a couple of your cretins and I ain't sorry one lick. You know you're goin' to rub me out so why not get to it?'

Cunningham drew closer.

'Have you heard the latest?'

'What would I hear?'

'My scouts inform me that your colonel and what looks like his entire gang have crossed the border into South Dakota and are reconnoitering in my direction. What do you make of that?'

Halliday was thoughtful. He'd claimed uninterest but it was not so. It seemed while a man was still breathing, he was curious.

Eventually he said, 'What's his interest in the Black Hills?'

Cunningham's face paled.

'I only found out recently. Of course I've known for a long time that someone was fomenting trouble over there, assisting the miners to flout the law, providing support and assistance to that Indian-killer at Crow Creek Stockade, Captain Harrelson. But it wasn't until the Bureau people stumbled on to my operation, and Dabney realized who I was, that I conducted my own investigation and discovered Dabney's involvement in the hills. On the wrong side, of course.'

'And what's your side? Sellin' rifles to Indians to kill Americans with?'

'How did you know. . . ?' Cunningham paused, shrugged. 'What does it matter? Yes, I'm the Sioux's friend, more so now I am aware of Dabney's perfidy than ever. Do you see him as the totally evil man he is now, Buckley? Surely you could no longer accept his word against mine on anything?'

Halliday was intrigued.

This man, crippled and dishonored by the country he'd served, had nursed his resentments all these years while working, not for the Sioux as he claimed, but rather against the Army. That was how Halliday saw it. He'd cut himself off from all contact with his old career, his own kind of people. Yet when Halliday had blundered into his life on a murder mission, Cunningham had learned about his connection with the 25th and had felt the compulsive need to be believed, understood, perhaps even absolved from the guilt which Uncle Sam's court martial had burdened him with.

He almost pitied him.

'If Dabney's doin' whatever you say, then he's all the way wrong. I don't hold with makin' things worse for the Indians than they already are. That's as far as I'm prepared to go.'

Cunningham smiled. 'That's quite a long way, Buckley.'

'What now?'

Cunningham's gaze turned distant. 'I have many things on my mind right now, I'll need time to think.'

'Are you goin' to goddamn kill me?'

'Only time will tell. Take him back to the brig, men, but treat him well. You're a strange man, Buck Halliday, but a man. You remind me of myself before . . . before . . .'

He was off someplace in the past now, reliving it, hurting, hating. The men escorted Halliday back across the compound, where he sighted the ugly mule and the wild eyed broomtail smooching through the corral fence. His only reaction was that, seeing as both were males, their behaviour seemed pretty sick to him. But then, didn't some say it was a sick world?

CHAPTER 8

TRUE HATE

Dust clouds rose ragged against the moon as the last of the laden wagons flanked by the outriders rumbled through the gates. They rolled off along the rough track which passed for a trail which wound away from the Fort westward through the shadow-rumpled badlands.

Parapet sentries standing the dogwatch followed the wagons' slow progress as they'd done with those leaving earlier. The men traded silent stares and nervously lit up pipes and cigarettes before returning their attention to the lamplit compound below.

This shipment was the big one.

Although the Fort had been trading weapons to the Sioux for some time as the Black Hills wars heated up, tonight's cargo was the largest by far. Soon every last scout, gunman and driver would be quitting the Fort to ride after the train, which by then would be strung out along the main trail. A mere skeleton crew would be left behind to man the Fort while Major Cunningham personally supervized the turnover of the rifles to his Indian allies.

Why wouldn't lowly rank and filers be jittery on such an occasion? They still had protection here, but for how long?

They'd never been left so depleted in strength at the Fort before. Every man was well aware of the increasing presence of Bureau scouts in the region, which could be alarming at any time, even more so now. It seemed to the hired help and the sentries that ever since Halliday had been captured, then escaped, they had been virtually overlooked as events rushed toward a climax.

The feeling was that Halliday should have been shot just the moment he was hauled back. Hadn't he staged an escape that had cost several lives? The bastard had killed Sergei. Shooting would be too good for him. For both of them; Halliday and the scurvy looking Mexican he'd picked up someplace.

Abilene and Cade were both in murderous tempers over the Halliday affair.

They'd wanted the big gunner dead from the outset. They'd read his brand correctly. They couldn't figure what more the bastard had to do before he got to shake hands with the firing squad.

Sobering reflections were interrupted yet again by a commotion in the yard. Devil and that ugly mule were at it again, trotting up and down the mustang's fence, nuzzling one another through the railings.

Abilene emerged from the stables to stand in a patch of moonlight to watch the horseplay.

Smoke trickled slowly from the killer's thin lips as he took out his .45 and checked the loads. He didn't consider crossing the yard and blasting both mustang and mule, even though the idea appealed. Other matters took precedent in his thinking right now. Halliday's crash-out, Sergei's brutal end, the big shipment going ahead as planned despite all this . . . Cunningham's puzzling behaviour. The whole mix seemed wrong on this, their biggest night. Abilene, top gun at the Fort now, felt the full weight of responsibility had fallen across his shoulders.

But if Cunningham was not as clear-headed and decisive as he should be tonight, then he sure was.

Those thoughts were his companions as he silently he made his cat-footed way past the corrals, pausing a moment to stare coldly at the big ugly dun hanging its head over the half-door.

They'd discovered Halliday's half-starved cayuse out by the devil's marbles following the manhunt. If Abilene had his way he'd shoot the animal along with Halliday and the Mex. He would do all three for free and for nothing. He only needed the nod.

He continued on through moonlight and shadow until reaching the main yard. He stopped to stare across at the rectangle of light spilling from the brig window.

What he saw didn't improve his mood one lick.

He could see the Mex perched on a bench coaxing discordant note music from paper and comb. Halliday was visible seated on the bunk, one arm behind his head, sucking on one of the colonel's cigars.

Abilene reached down and loosened the Colt .45 in its holster. His teeth showed but he wasn't smiling. Who could understand Cunningham tonight? he brooded. There was a suspicion that his wife had engineered Halliday's breakout; the man had butchered Sergei like a mongrel dog; now he was back behind bars yet Cunningham had taken no action. Why was the big bastard still breathing?

He crossed the yard in shadow and in total silence, intending at least to throw a scare into the prisoners. But no sooner was he in place, crouched below the barred window, than a familiar voice drawled:

'Yeah, what you want, low-life?'

Halliday hadn't even turned his head as he spoke. Abilene's face burned as he rose to full height. He'd made no sound as he approached, he was sure of it. It seemed that every time they made contact, Halliday got to achieve an edge.

'It's maggot-check time,' he hissed back.

'I like that,' said Halliday. 'You like his brand of wit, wetback?'

Caraso rolled rogue eyes at the face beyond the bars. He smiled uneasily. '*Buenos noches*, Señor Abilene.' He was suddenly anxious. 'You do not come to shoot us, no?'

' 'Course he ain't, knucklehead,' Halliday grunted, swinging big boots to the floor. He stood, squinting out at Abilene over his cigar as though lining him up in gunsights. 'We'd be goners long back if they'd meant to shoot us. So there's a reason we're still alive. Ain't that so, small-time?'

Abilene thrust his gunbarrel between the bars.

Caraso yipped and dived under the bunk. Halliday's smoke-wreathed expression didn't change.

The gun slowly lowered.

'You'll keep, maggot.' Abilene fought to keep his voice steady. 'Just believe this. You're gonna die. And when it happens, it'll be me pullin' the trigger. Bet on it.'

'If I had five dollars for every loser that was goin' to put me in the . . .'

But Abilene heard no more as he strode away. He was mad all over again, mad enough in fact to head for Cunningham's quarters after checking at the mess hall to ensure that the men were preparing for the night ride.

He found the major slumped behind his desk. A map of the region was spread before him. He'd been outlining the proposed route of the shipment with a black grease pencil. The desk lamp shadowed his face as he leaned back and glanced up.

'Can't sleep, boy?'

'Who sleeps?'

'You're testy. What's on your mind?'

Abilene told him. Halliday. Dabney's scouts. The huge risks involved in taking all the guns through in the one major shipment rather than filter them through in dribs and drabs as was their custom. Cunningham could take his pick.

Cunningham was calm and reassuring. He knew exactly what he was doing, he stated. Dabney was out there; the Sioux needed the guns now; he was ready for a showdown.

There was no need for Abilene to fret – the boss

had everything well in hand.

'What about Halliday?' the gunman demanded. 'Lettin' that mucker live is bad for morale, Major. The men are stewing about it. Are you really serious about him going with us tonight?'

'Of course.'

'Why, for God's sake?'

Cunningham's tone grew confidential. He tapped his map.

'Abilene, this is our biggest operation ever, I don't need to tell you that. Dabney is at full strength and we know full well he wants to destroy me whatever else he does or doesn't do.' He tapped the pencil on the desk. 'Halliday is his man, he hired him to kill me, he's valuable to Dabney for reasons we're all aware of.' He smiled as he leaned back. 'Hostage, man, hostage. This is going to be a showdown between me and Dabney and I'm arming myself with every weapon I can lay my hands on. You understand now?'

Abilene just stared.

He'd never been able to figure the major. Crippled yet proud, strong but vulnerable, open then unfathomable. How did you read a man like that?

He gusted breath through his nostrils and slapped his holster. Times like this he felt he should quit. The only thing stopping him was that he truly believed that, despite all Cunningham's weaknesses and short-comings, the man was destined to go all the way to the top in the Black Hills and he meant to stay on for the ride.

The gunman quit the room soon after, appeased if

not totally satisfied. He left Cunningham leaning back in his chair, no longer smiling, his expression dark and unreadable.

'Halliday,' he murmured aloud in the silence.

He'd lied to his gunman, of course. It was only remotely possible that Halliday might have any value at all as a hostage. That would depend upon how events of the next twenty-four hours went. The real reason Halliday was still alive after what he'd done was so strange that a man like Abilene would never understand. Maybe nobody would.

Cunningham craved Halliday's understanding.

During his years of self-imposed exile as his hatred for the Army drew him into supporting the Sioux, Cunningham had had no contact with any officer, past or present.

Halliday slam-banging into his life, and emerging from his files as an officer, gentleman and hero of the 25th, had reactivated his hunger for understanding and acceptance as the cruelly wronged leader of men he'd been before Vicksburg.

Cunningham felt if he could convince just one former luminary of the regiment of his innocence, it would be a great achievement. He was still determined to achieve this end even if Halliday's actions were making it increasingly difficult to keep him alive.

There was another reason also.

Cunningham groaned in pain as he hauled himself out of his seat and dropped into his rubber-tyred wheelchair. Cruising silently down lamplit corridors, he paused at a half-opened doorway to peer in.

His wife slept with her hair a dark cloud upon the pillow. He would need to wake her shortly for the journey. The shipment with which he expected to achieve so much would signal the completion of his major arms deal with the Sioux. Armed with the best of modern weaponry, he was certain the Indians would triumph in the undeclared war in the Black Hills. He also envisioned the destruction of Dabney, ten years overdue, and the resolution of his doubts about Lu Nin.

Cunningham turned through the next door. His wife's dressing room was immaculately neat, as always. Wheeling to a blanket box in a corner, he raised the lid, looked in.

It was still there. She hadn't dared try to get rid of it yet.

He drew out the black silk dress, the one with the short puffed sleeves and fitted bodice. Turning it over in in his hands, he found the hole in the right sleeve. It was round and frayed at the edges, unmistakably a bullet hole to the eye of a man who had seen so many.

He knew someone had assisted Halliday the night of the breakout. Someone had unlocked his cell door and released him. Sentries had glimpsed a slender figure running from the pumphouse gate during Halliday's escape, had fired at him. Or her. Cunningham had once been betrayed by an officer and a superior at Vicksburg. It was like a knife twisting in his guts, the fear that he may have also been betrayed by the woman he loved.

*

Halliday lowered his weight into the saddle and patted the dun's neck. The compound blazed with torchlight and bustling activity surrounded him as the remainder of the Fort's personnel prepared to take to the trail. It was anticipated they would overtake the wagon column some time before daybreak.

Rifles glinted, saddle leathers creaked, throats were nervously cleared in the chill night.

This was the big one.

There wasn't an American, Indian or Chinese amongst them not fully aware of the dangers of the situation. Their enemies of the Bureau were in the Black Hills in strength. Despite this the major still intended running the Winchester shipment through to Crazy Horse's lieutenant, Red Man, to enable the Sioux first to sack Crow Creek Stockade before unleashing their full fury upon the miners.

Everything that had gone before had been mere preparation for this. The men were uneasy but drew reassurance from the almost stalwart picture presented by Cunningham now as he was wheeled into the yard, waving and smiling on his way to the corrals.

The major had to say goodbye to Devil.

Buck arched an eyebrow at a jittery Caraso. The Mexican's mule was acting up, plainly wanting to stay behind with its brand-new best friend.

'At last you and that dumb critter are of one mind,' he remarked. 'Neither of you wants to go, although it's yellow funk with you while it's true love with him.'

'I am not afraid, *muchacha*, and it is evil of you to say that Joachim and the mustang . . .'

'All right, let's shut up and listen,' cut in Abilene,

approaching on foot. 'You two will be escorted by men with orders to shoot to kill all around you every mile, and you know, I only hope you do try something.' He signalled to the gateman. 'All right, Tutt, open her up. You about ready, Major?'

Cunningham didn't hear, what with the gates creaking open and the mustang making such a racket. As Halliday and Caraso started forward with their escort, Devil began rearing and pawing at his fence, acting up a treat both because the major was saying goodbye and the mule was plainly going with him.

Everyone was either annoyed or amused by the display. All but Halliday.

His eyes were now focused on the sweep of tortured landscape appearing slowly before him as the gates opened to their full extent.

At that moment, he was not thinking about rifles, Indians, obsessive enemies, handsome females, or the racket. Halliday was again thinking freedom, scenting it and breathing it while only half-listening as Cunningham barked an order.

'Open that corral gate, Abilene,' he said emotionally as Devil was like to turn himself inside out. 'I've got to soothe him, can't leave him like this.'

'You reckon that's such a smart idea, Major?'

Abilene would plug the broomtail without a second thought. But Cunningham was insistent, so the gate was unlatched and he entered the corral as he had done many times before; he was the only one Devil would let near him.

The trembling stallion came to him and onlookers

marvelled at the rapport evident between man and beast.

Until Joachim brayed emotionally.

The effect was electric. With an answering whicker, Devil swung away from Cunningham and was through the gate in a flash, striking it with a shoulder to slam it back into Abilene, who was knocked off his feet.

The mule promptly pitched Caraso off on to his head, creating instant panic as he attempted to plough right through the massed horsemen to join his 'friend'.

A flash of farce in the middle of high drama – and only Halliday saw its potential.

He was mounted. He was cooler than he'd ever been. The gates stood open, there was scarcely a man uninvolved in the uproar. Through the billowing dust the smells of the open country beyond the gates was a heady drug.

His heels slammed horsehide.

He kicked so hard the dun almost went down on its knees. It recovered instantly to take one huge leap forward which carried them past two fallen horses, a shouting Indian pinned by one leg, the careering surrey holding Lu Nin and her driver, and a wild eyed Chinese with a rifle in his hands who seemed to be trying to shoot the mule, Devil, or both.

Two men blocked the gateway. Halliday charged directly at them. Their guns were coming up as they saw their danger. Too late. Halliday plunged between them, his horse's pumping shoulders slamming against them and sending them flying end over end as the barrel-chested dun really hit his stride.

Lying over the powerful neck as the first shots came, Halliday heard the howls of confusion turn to shouts of rage in his dust.

'Come on, you bag of bones!' he yelled in the horse's ear. 'This is the one that counts.'

The horse lifted his gait. A bullet whistled between the animal's legs, another smacked into the saddle, missing Halliday's right thigh by a fraction. He felt the exhilaration rise as they hammered the man-made wagon trail, heard bullets plop harmlessly behind him now as they opened up the gap.

Halliday's heart thudded in his chest. He was grinning like a wolf. He'd outrun those sons of bitches afoot, he told himself joyously. How could they expect to catch him with the best horse in the West beneath him?

He hammered on with the horse's silken mane streaming in his face like the wind.

Eventually the column was back in formation and beginning to make good time along the trail. The lights of the Fort were now but a dim glow on the northeastern horizon behind and riders were beginning to light cigarettes and talk to one another again following the escape.

Everyone was referring to it as such now even though Abilene and several scouts were still off hunting the runaway.

Nobody expected the searchers to return with Halliday again, either dead or alive. Not this time. He'd taken off like a bobcat with its tail afire, like someone who mightn't break off for a smoke before he hit Nebraska, maybe Kansas, even.

A different sort of sidekick might have exulted in a companion's courage and good fortune, but Teo Caraso was not that sort.

'I am surely the poorest of *hombres*,' he confided to an uncaring moon. 'Apart from my sister in Sonora, all I have in my sad life is my mule and my *amigo*. My mule' – he paused to look down at his animal's ugly head, – 'disgraces me. My great friend runs away and leaves me to the mercies of my enemies. Do you listen, Lord? No, please do not answer. Even you I fear would only lie.'

'Shuddup or I'll plug you!' snarled the man at his side, who was sure he'd cracked a rib back at the Fort. And Caraso fell silent, shifting his weight in the saddle just to make the load heavier and more uncomfortable for his unforgiven fool of a mule.

The major dragged his bleak stare away from the Mexican to look across at his wife in the surrey. Lu Nin dabbed at her eyes. Cunningham turned ahead. He wondered if he would ever learn the truth about them . . . or if he might already know.

Halliday was feeling great.

Halliday was feeling pretty good.

Halliday was feeling fairly OK, all things considered.

A rare tree showed up ahead atop a grassy knoll and the rider steered for it, swinging down in the welcome shade. The horse blew noisily and shook out its mane. Halliday took out the last of

Cunningham's Cubans and patted his pockets for his vestas.

A frown cut between black brows as he fired up the cigar and took a deep draw.

Sometimes he really didn't understand himself, and this was such a time. Here he was, free as a jaybird, unscathed, unharried, his own good mount beneath him and thousands of square miles of open land and sky to call his own, yet here he was feeling merely OK when by rights he should be ten feet tall and laughing.

What was it? Why did he feel uneasy when he should feel the exact opposite?

His gaze played restlessly over what would have to be the most grotesque landscape in the entire country. Nothing to see, not even a bird. Yet the badlands were anything but empty. Out there someplace was a sometime partner and a woman he'd thought he felt something for. There was even a strange and driven man who'd spared his life unaccountably more than once, and for whom he suspected he felt something, he wasn't sure what.

And that wasn't all.

The badlands region was anything but desolate and empty today but rather was peopled with weapon smugglers, Bureau hellions, likely even Sioux and mad miners; who could be sure?

So much activity out there, so much peace and quiet here under his lonesome cottonwood. He gazed up through the leaves at a badlands sun marching across the sky. He wondered what scenes it might set upon tonight if events were simply allowed to run their course without any interference from the one man who just might have the ability to stave off chaos.

Someone about his size.

He glanced south one more time. Nothing down there but more of the same of what he had right here, sleepy tranquillity and badlands silence.

He hadn't made any hard-edged decisions by the time he threw a leg across his horse and tipped his hat low over his eyes. Just an awareness of what he felt he could do, should do, maybe even might do . . . if he was crazy enough to try. . . .

The horse moved out of the tree shade at his touch and the sun struck like a hammer across Halliday's shoulders. He leaned ahead.

CHAPTER 9

DOGS OF WAR

The gunmen dismounted and strode towards the big Sibley tent pitched on the slope amongst the conifers. Rifle-toting sentries snapped to attention at their approach. They didn't salute, but had they done so it would hardly have seemed out of place. In the field, the colonel ran things pretty much as he had done during the war. Dabney was yet to come out openly and declare that cold young gunmen with their clean-shaven faces understood the reality of the situation.

Men would die today, widows would weep, goals would be achieved and defeat's acrid poison tasted. That was war.

The Bureau's campground was strategically placed roughly halfway between Council Rock Crossing to the east and Crow Creek Stockade on the Singing River to the west.

The original plan to ambush the gunrunners at

the crossing had been altered by Dabney upon realizing just how strong Cunningham's party was. It was
also known now that that Cunningham himself was
accompanying his wagons, which called for greater
caution and care.

Dabney had quit the safety and security of the base
in Wichita for the north country with the intention
of surprising Cunningham and destroying him in
order to ensure that the Winchesters did not fall into
the hands of Gall, Crazy Horse, Red Man or others of
their breed.

Ever since learning of the true strength of the Fort
party which had been sighted in the early morning
far out in the badlands by his outriders, Dabney had
been working at a furious pace, plotting, planning,
issuing directives, poring over his maps, slugging
down the occasional bracer to quieten his nerves.

As had become his habit, he delegated much of
the actual practical work to Cole and Petrie.
Although cast from much the same mould as many
others of his hand-picked Bureau personnel, the two
had long since proven themselves a cut above the
rest. In the past Dabney had blooded the pair of
them in several underhand deals and high-danger
enterprises, and they had come through every time.

He'd been reluctantly preparing to assign them to
the highly dangerous task of assassinating Cunningham several weeks earlier, before the sudden winds
of good fortune had blown his way. Halliday's timely
surfacing out of his past had been interpreted by a
superstitious Dabney as the omen of good fortune
he'd been searching for.

That soldier he'd stumbled upon fighting for his life in that murky smoke-ghosted back alley in Atlanta – the man whose life he'd saved on a mere whim – had proven a godsend. Difficult, aggressive and unpredictable – certainly. But Halliday would never let him down, nor had he even complained about the way in which he was being forced to discharge his debt.

Halliday's sense of morality left the former Union cavalryman officer intensely grateful yet bemused. Personally, Dabney wouldn't acknowledge any responsibility under any circumstance without someone holding a gun at his head. Yet Halliday was prepared to go against conscience and revulsion and do what was demanded of him, simply because he was a man who believed a blood debt must be repaid.

At a vital time like this it did him good to reflect on Halliday and all the others who had proven themselves so reliable 'in the field'. Dabney utilized that phrase often, rolling it off his tongue, as though he believed in courage in the field of battle as the supreme characteristic for the true fighting man. Yet during the war days when a soldier in the field himself, Colonel Dabney had often been more treacherous than brave, and only luck and a razor-edged intelligence had at times saved him from court martial or firing squad.

The two riders delivered their report. Everything was in order up at the stockade, and Cunningham's column was now visible out in the badlands from their scouts' lookout position atop lofty Harney Peak.

There were also reports from the men they'd put

into the Belle Fouche and Cheyenne Rivers regions, he was told.

'We were able to work our way in reasonably close to the column, even belly-wriggling between the enemy outriders at times,' Cole said with obvious pride. 'Although one varmint did spot us . . . right, Petrie?'

'Spotted us . . . almost got to raise the alarm,' Petrie replied, standing with boots wide planted and hands licked behind his back. Then he actually grinned. 'Then my Bowie sunk into his backbone and he didn't say one damned word.'

They stood before him basking in his approval. And Dabney was genuinely proud of them both. Yet in the same moment he was thinking just how chilling and unnerving his young killers were. His fighting force were all military rejects, and he could easily understand why they never made the grade in uniform. They were mavericks – like himself. He found himself reflecting on how different the breed was from Halliday. The big man was immensely difficult yet was straight as a gunbarrel. He was no slinking killer like his West Point butcher boys.

'Numbers?' he asked briskly.

The reports affirmed that, as suspected, the gunrunners were travelling at full strength. And there was a puzzling yet interesting footnote; a prisoner traveling with Cunningham was the same strange odd-ball who'd visited headquarters in Wichita in search of Halliday, one Teo Caraso.

He asked about Halliday and was startled upon learning that the big man was not with the

Cunningham party.

'We figure he must be dead, sir,' Petrie said with some satisfaction.

'Cunningham alive and Halliday dead,' commented Cole, rubbing it in. 'Not exactly the situation we wanted at this moment, Colonel?'

'Get out!' Dabney said in sudden rage. Halliday missing? He couldn't believe the man was dead. Which only left one possible alternative explanation. The big man had quit on him. Welched on their bargain. How could he have misjudged him so badly?

'Have my horse and escort readied. I'm going to check on the stockade. I'll leave you men in command along this piece of trail. Remember, Cunningham is to be observed at all times but in no way hindered until I so order.'

'Sir!' the two said in unison, clicking their heels.

'One more thing. Anything on the Sioux?'

'Large party reported coming down the Singing River and possibly making for the stockade an hour ago,' Petrie furnished.

Dabney permitted himself a tight grin. Good. It looked as if the elaborate battle plan might be working as smoothly as a piece of Swiss clockwork. And why not? It was his plan and he'd spent much time developing it.

Riding through the sun-dappled woods a short time later, flanked by his heavily-armed escort, Dabney found himself brooding about Halliday again.

Angrily he switched his thoughts to Cunningham. His face hardened. It was only by coincidence that the two former commanders from the 25th Cavalry had locked horns again under strange circumstances here in the Dakotas. In his wide-ranging occupations of intelligence gathering, mostly legitimate, and wheeling and dealing under the cover of his reputation and impressive record, mostly highly suspect, Dabney trod a high-risk path. He'd survived because of his cleverness. The way he organized all his affairs and enterprises, if something should ever go wrong – as it sometimes did – nothing could ever be traced back to him. He called powerful men his friends and traded heavily on his war record, which remained largely unsullied.

But Cunningham cast a long shadow.

Not only did the man have every legitimate reason to want him dead, and obviously now had the capability of achieving this end, the man also had damning knowledge of that ugly incident in the Vicksburg campaign which, if made public and proven before a court martial, could still shatter Dabney's reputation overnight and even might land him behind bars or before a military firing squad.

He shivered involuntarily.

None of these things must be allowed to happen. And only a man who thought genuinely large-scale as he did, he congratulated himself, could design and engineer an engagement which would ensure both the destruction of all his enemies in this region, including not only the gunrunners and much of the the Sioux, but Major Cunningham himself.

Dabney had long anticipated this overdue showdown and had already taken strategic steps to ensure his victory when he and Cunningham clashed – should Halliday fail in his mission to take him out.

The enemies would meet in the Black Hills when and where Dabney planned they would. He'd planned it down to the smallest detail – the trap, the avalanche, the total destruction.

He would wind up with Cunningham's weapons and the Sioux would be left hanging – easy game for his men and the miners he supported. Who needed Halliday, when it came right down to cases?

He felt even surer of himself when his party topped out the ridge overlooking the cleared hill upon which Crow Creek Stockade stood as the symbol of military authority over what was currently the most potentially explosive geographical point in the entire West.

The outpost appeared deserted. Gates creaked open in the wind and empty windows overlooked deserted parade grounds.

Considering the fact that the Bureau was a rock-solid supporter of the stockade's Captain Harrelson, the C.O. charged with the weighty responsibility of trying to keep the miners out of the Black Hills and the Sioux from breaking out into open war over their intrusions, Dabney's reaction to this desolate sight was puzzling.

The man wore a triumphal grin as his party melted back into the Black Hills' sheltering conifers.

The sound of a shot carried faintly to the column as they were taking the wagons through the shallow waters of the fording.

Immediately Cunningham called a halt and the six wagons and the outriders quickly scrambled to take up defensive positions in the brush and rocks flanking the trail, as Cade and Abilene went racing off to reconnoiter.

Teo Caraso took the opportunity to dismount and massage his chafing backside. Having deliberately subjected his mule to a steady tongue-lashing for its unseemly behaviour at the Fort, the critter had gotten back at him by assuming a gait halfway between a disjointed trot and an ungainly walk that jarred every bone in the rider's scrawny body, particularly those he used for sitting on.

The Mexican kept rolling his eyes as everyone stared northwards at the broken-backed ridge from where the shot had come. While everyone else was awaiting the outcome of the diversion with a gun in his fist, he was unarmed and at the mercy of any bloodthirsty band of brigands who might come churning into sight.

It was a fact of life that Caraso's courage was at best an uncertain thing, even when armed and with Halliday and his lightning Colts to back him up.

He wished Halliday were around right now even if he had vowed never to speak to the man again for making his spectacular break and leaving him behind.

'Do you wish for a drink?'

He looked up at Lu Nin. She proffered a metal water canteen.

He grabbed it and tipped the cold water to his parched lips, for Abilene had ordered that he receive nothing from anybody other than the occasional clip around the ears from him.

He hated Abilene as only a lowly Mexican horse thief could hate an outsized big-head who fancied himself as God's gift to the gun trade. But of course he also hated Cunningham, the Indians, the Chinese and the gringo gunrunners. He hated their horses and the very air they breathed. Hate was stoking Caraso's boilers today as he viewed the probably fatal position he now found himself in when his only crime had been to risk life and limb to help his great swell *amigo*, Halliday.

In his heart, he hoped Halliday might be still alive. Preferably up to his neck in an ants' nest with naked, luscious women pouring honey over his head, but alive.

Then he sighed. If Halliday died then he would not have a friend in the world but for his sister Francesca, who despised him.

Maybe a lousy, rotten, leave-a-man-hanging pard was better than no pard at all.

'*Gracias*,' he said, returning the canteen. And blinked in surprise to see tears in the eyes of the lovely Lu Nin. '*Señora*, you too are afraid?'

'I fear for your friend.'

Bells tinkled in Teo Caraso's skull as strange computations began to arrange themselves in his brainbox. For he had lost count of the number of women who'd wept over Halliday, and nine times out of ten, they wept for but one reason. Love. The subject about which Halliday understood nothing, or so he believed in the wake of the Clara Cable affair.

131

He'd not mentioned Clara Cable of Paradise County on this venture. He only hoped to live long enough to discuss Halliday's beautiful and strong-minded ex under better circumstances with his 'friend'.

'*Señor?*'

He came back to the present.

'You?' he heard himself say. His brows elevated. 'You care for Señor Halliday?'

She looked away and he shot a glance back at Cunningham's rig. The man was paying them no attention as he sat alongside his driver watching for his men, a big heavy service revolver dangling from his fist.

And Caraso saw that the cripple was unafraid. He could scent cowardice as easily as courage, and this man whom life had treated too carelessly was surely one of the brave ones.

His attention returned to Lu Nin. Before he could speak, hoofbeats drummed on hard ground and he sighted three riders coming back from the broken-backed ridge, Abilene, Cade and one of their Sioux scouts.

The report was matter-of-fact; the scout had clashed with a Bureau rider and put a bullet in his shoulder before the man escaped.

To Caraso's surprise, Cunningham seemed relieved. 'I was starting to grow uneasy,' he explained. 'We knew they were in the region, we know their strength, and yet we've barely sighted them. At least we now know they're close, and forearmed is fore-warned. In which case, we'll get under way again.'

'This sad one will travel with me, my husband,' Lu Nin called. 'He is too sore to ride further on the mule.'

Cunningham merely shrugged indifferently as he drove by. That was how come a relaxing Caraso found himself seated on soft leather cushions and travelling in comparative luxury as they quit the crossing area and drove deeper into the Black Hills.

'You are too kind, *señora*.'

'Would you care to use some of my perfume?'

What a dampener!

'Would you care for something to mend your breaking heart, fair lady?' he retorted.

He saw the barb strike home. Lu Nin navigated the rig round a hole in the trail, glanced at him sideways.

'What manner of man is he, really, Teo?'

'The very worst.'

'Will he . . . will he come back for me?'

'You might well ask will the mule and Devil ever start a family of their own?'

Lu Nin's eyes turned misty and Caraso, immediately repentant, reached out to pat her hand.

A quirt cut stingingly across the back of his neck.

'Get your dirty paws off of the lady, wetback,' hissed Abilene, drawing alongside. 'B'God, but you've got some gall, takin' liberties with a respectable lady when you've got one foot in the grave.' He poked him with the quirt then flipped his sombrero back with it. 'You do know what's going on, don't you, dummy? We're expecting big trouble before we're through today, but we aim to deliver our guns and finish the Bureau once and for all. But when the shooting starts, who will be a sitting duck without a shooter? How many guesses do you want, boy?'

'Leave him be,' Lu Nin defended. Abilene rode on ahead with a cruel grin, but he'd spoiled the moment for Teo Caraso. He would have said the rosary if he could only remember how it went. He must get a gun someplace.

Red Man the Sioux had learned young and early the value of patience, of not rushing in first and fretting about consequences later. He might never have heard the White Eyes' phrase, 'look before you leap', but he'd rarely breached that rule and wasn't about to do so today, tempting though it might be.

Red Man was prepared to wait and watch until it hurt.

Times like this, the youthful Sioux leader found himself craving the more experienced counsel of Sitting Bull, Two Moons, Gall or Crazy Horse – who was really about as crazy as a fox. But they were otherwise occupied in the ongoing battles with the miners when the smoke signal alerted the Kree Point camp that the stockade had been abandoned.

This was so obviously a lie or some grim jest, that initially Red Man remained at the stronghold and sent two scouts down to investigate.

The Army's outpost on the slopes above Singing River north of River Bend and the Red Pines escarpment, had been there for years and never played a larger or more hated role in Indian affairs than recently.

The Army was supposed to be impartial in the worsening conflict between the Sioux and the ever increasing flood of check-shirted miners prepared to ignore all treaties and come take what they wanted with washpan, pickaxe and gun.

This was a grim joke.

For every miner to receive a rap over the knuckles by Captain Harrelson, half a dozen Sioux died. Harrelson was a crook, an opportunist, an Indian-hater and a disgrace to the uniform he was supposed to honor.

But the man was also a fighter, hard as nails and didn't seem to have a quitting bone in his rawboned body. Why would he quit when the Sioux had been quiet for some time and the captain appeared to be thriving and amassing a personal fortune out of the misery and bloodshed that was life in the Black Hills?

But the scouts returned with the startling confirmation that Crow Creek did indeed appear to be deserted, and Red Man and his warriors were up and riding within minutes.

They'd been lying concealed in the shadow of White Rock Ridge, watching the silent stockade for over an hour without catching one flicker of life, before Red Man finally decided he had been patient and prudent long enough.

No need to call for volunteers; every buck was eager to go check at first hand, despite the fact that this could still prove to be an elaborate trap.

But it wasn't.

When Red Man's nephew returned from his reconnoiter a short time later, it was to report that the stockade was as deserted as it looked. Not even a trooper's dog left down there, not one worthwhile piece of sign to indicate other than that the whole company had struck off through the deep woods to the northwest, possibly making for Rapid City.

They occupied the sturdy rock-and-log stockade warily and suspiciously, but soon were beginning to relax and rejoice.

The Bluecoats had run on the very day the tribes were expecting their biggest ever shipment of weapons from the Sioux's most honored friend, Army-hating Major Cunningham, and the Sioux scouts had kept Red Man informed all day on the convoy's slow but sure approach from badlands to river crossings to the very hills themselves.

Naturally the major must hear of this astonishing piece of good fortune as quickly as possible.

Cunningham proved initially as suspicious as the Sioux had been on hearing the news, sent Abilene and a squad of his best scouts ahead to double check the stockade area as the column wended its steadier way through the climbing landscape.

The scouts found nothing untoward; they were not meant to.

By mid-afternoon, grim Crow Creek Stockade presented a bustling picture of colorful activity as feathered Sioux and gunrunners mingled within and without its four, needle-tipped walls, breaking open crates of gleaming rifles, uncorking the occasional bottle, celebrating what already appeared to be the major turning point in the long struggle against what a smiling Cunningham chose to describe as 'the forces of militant darkness and murderous bigotry'.

This was the confounding scene which greeted the eyes of the big man in the black shirt who wriggled his way on his belly through the brush atop the granite bluffs flanking the eastern rim to part a clump of arrow-grass with his hands and stare down.

Halliday's was not the only unseen eye gazing down into Singing River basin.

CHAPTER 10

THE BIG GUNDOWN

It wasn't his nature to be patient. Buck Halliday could be infinitely patient and crafty when stalking or infiltrating, as he had just proven here. But when forced just to lie around under a blanket of concealing brush, scratching his head and frowning with concentration, it went hard against the grain and caused his big thigh muscles to ache from the inactivity.

Yet he stuck to it like a chess champion contemplating the actions of the enemy, which while appearing as normal as blueberry pie on the surface, still touched off little alarm buzzers of danger.

Once again he considered the playboard: Indians and gunrunners occupying the stockade; no outward signs of bloody battle; not one live Bluecoat or even a dead one to meet the eye. Add late afternoon sunlight sheening the conifers and pines as though to bestow the final touch of normality over a scene that this veteran found about as normal as a plate of scorpion soup.

So he lay there as the sun slid down the sky and his restless gaze never ceased to play over basin, river, cliff walls, hills, sky and buttes until his head was aching and his eyes turned gritty.

Then he saw it.

It took the eagle eye of a scout to detect the faint irregularity in the upsloping grass patches leading from the dip beyond the stockade on the northern side, up to the heroic mass of talus abutting the squat broken butte, whose bulk blocked off from sight a large section of the red pine hillsides beyond River Bend.

He blinked and looked again.

No doubt about it.

Something had disturbed the grass along some kind of rough line, which upon squinting his eyes, he found he could follow almost from stockade to guardian butte. Something had damaged the grass earlier in the day and the hot sun had dried it out to leave a whitish trace.

It might not be much, yet it seemed a great deal to a man convinced that something here in Crow Creek Stockade, named after the piddling little tributary which wound down to join the river close by, stank like week-old fish.

Too bad he could not alert Cunningham, but to have tried would surely prove fatal. Right now, as he eased back from the rim, he knew he also didn't want to alert anybody until he knew both what was taking place here and just what type of a game was being played.

*

The darkening surface of the river broke silently, a dripping head emerged slowly, vanished quickly.

Trotting side by side along the bank as they made their way back towards the stockade, were three Cunningham scouts returning from a reconnoiter of the northern end of the basin where Singing River swept by Yellow Butte. Despite the festive air at the stockade where the celebration of the post's uncontested capture was still in progress, both Cunningham and Red Man were still taking precautions. Captain Harrelson, four cannon and upwards of forty troopers had vanished without trace, and the scouting parties were returning still without having figured out where the soldiers had gone or why.

By the time the dripping figure emerged again beneath a shoulder of the bank some fifty yards downstream towards the base of the mesa, the scouts had vanished inside the stockade where lamps and torches were being lit in the deepening dusk.

Halliday sucked in a deep breath as his narrowed gaze played over the steep grass slope before him which was now being slowly swallowed by darkness. For one brief moment, and for the final time, he asked himself just what in hell he thought he was doing, alone, unarmed, unaligned and dripping wet – nosing into something so dangerous that no man with half a brain would touch it with a barge pole.

He knew what he was doing, and why. That out of his system, he spent several minutes smothering himself from head to toe with black river sediment.

He then wriggled over the high bank and proceeded to snake his way through the upslope, determined to find that discolored grass line in the darkness.

Singing sounded from the stockade and his sharp ears picked up less identifiable sounds from somewhere higher upon the mesa.

Surprisingly, the lighter colored line of dead grass stood out quite clearly when he came belly-wriggling up to it from the river side. He rested momentarily then began to dig. He didn't have to go down far in disturbed soil to grasp the slim cables buried there. He hauled them up and studied them, puzzled at first. He'd seen such wires a thousand times during the war. They were employed to carry electrical impulses to explosives in demolition work.

He gazed towards the stockade where the line of the wires stretched away to his right, then swung left where it climbed up the face of the mesa.

Suddenly everything began to make a chilling kind of sense. An empty fort, the enemy flooding in, someone leaning on a plunger well out of harm's way . . . an entire stockade going up in one mighty roar taking everyone within with it.

The impulse to raise the alarm was quickly quashed. Right at that very moment the Bluecoats – it had to be them at the other end of these wires – could be ready to touch off whatever they'd planted beneath the stockade's sturdy floorboards, and his raising Cain would surely see them set it off.

Which left him but one alternative.

Making his way swiftly to the base of the mesa, he began to climb.

Those sounds he'd heard earlier from this area grew louder as he warily approached the shadowy mesa top, but it wasn't until he cautiously raised his head above the rim that he realized the cause. Dark figures were in the process of removing brush covers from some three or four dully gleaming pieces of the gunmakers' craft. Army cannon, their menacing maws pointed south towards the stockade.

And looping over the rim not twenty feet to his right, the detonator cables.

Taking risks he couldn't believe in the taut minutes that followed, Halliday scouted the periphery of the mesa-top activity to make several vital discoveries. Atop the mesa were the cannon plus the all-important explosives plunger manned by maybe ten troopers. Barely visible behind a stone shoulder of the mesa some hundred feet below, out of sight of the stockade, the shadowy shapes of the main force were to be glimpsed assembling for battle.

The plan was plain. Set off the explosives, support it with cannon fire then send in the foot soldiers to mop up what was left. It was breathtaking in its audacity. And it was going to work like clockwork if somebody didn't do something.

No free cigar for guessing who that crazy somebody had to be.

Cutting back across the mesa top in a low crouch, in the direction of the bustling activity around the cannon, and the piles of shells and explosives the soldiers intended raining down on the stockade, the Sioux, the gunrunners and the Winchesters, Halliday was not a thinking man any longer. He was a soldier again, a lethal entity there, just one man against many, yet one man armed with the vital weapon of surprise – and a flint pocket lighter which might or might not prove to be waterproof.

Time he got himself a gun.

The trooper crossing from left to right across Halliday's line of vision never stood a chance. He was taken from behind, the head was twisted violently to one side, a dull crack and it was over.

Now Halliday had his gun. Almost as importantly, he also had a knife.

There were now but two men guarding the plunger. It must be neutralized first. Thrusting knife and gun through his belt, the mud-blackened figure came up behind the pair, reared up lightning fast, grabbed two heads in two big hands and brought them brutally together.

The troopers went down. But he'd been heard. There was no way he couldn't be. 'What the hell is going on over there?' someone hissed from the cannon line, and immediately Halliday glimpsed the dim silhouettes of figures rushing his way to investigate.

But his Bowie was in one hand by this, the lethal cables in the other. He slashed viciously, the wires parted and he was plunging away as a hoarse voice yelled, 'What? Halt or I shoot!'

Halliday ran. Nothing to be gained by stealth now. The unconscious men were found and he could feel the panic hit the enemy as they rushed this way and that trying to figure what it was they were up against.

143

Someone was calling down to the riverside for instructions while figures fanned out to search for the intruder.

But Halliday had doubled back on the mesa's east flank, was now crouched by the gunpowder stack, furiously working the wheel of his stubborn pocket flint with his thumb.

He could hear pounding steps rushing his way as the flint finally flared into life. He flicked it atop the pile, swung away towards the rim more swiftly than he'd moved in his life, took two huge strides then found himself airborne and sailing over that high rim as the crown of Yellow Mesa erupted like a volcano.

Then there was only darkness.

Sprawled unconscious in a huge rhododendron bush sprouting from inhospitable talus plating the flanks of the mesa, a smoke and mud-blackened Halliday missed it all. He didn't witness Harrelson's fatal indecision following the blast which took out his cannon, nor the counter-attack launched against the troopers by Red Man's Sioux, which was eventually backed up by Cunningham when a vicious battle of attrition roared and raged along the east bank of Singing River not a hundred yards from where his unconscious figure lay.

Maybe it was just as well that Halliday was lost in limbo while the slaughter continued, for he wouldn't have known who to root for.

Sure, he'd risked his neck against the troopers. But that action had been motivated by personal reasons. Two of them: Lu Nin and Caraso. There was no way he could have stood by and watched them die while he could do something to prevent it.

But that was as far as sentiment went. He had no more time for gunrunners and scalp-lifting Sioux than he did for a corrupt military, Dabney and his lousy Bureau. Or a bunch of hairy miners, if they were indeed involved.

Any idealism he may have once had was long gone. Mostly all he believed in now was excitement, action, women and freedom.

He was musing dazedly on all four when Teo Caraso and his stolen shotgun finally found him.

By then the battle was over and the banks of Singing River were littered with dead and wounded. There was skirmishing going on in the surrounding woods and up along the stream around Big Bend. But Cunningham had claimed victory following the death of Captain Harrelson and Dabney's abrupt flight.

The combined force of Harrelson's troopers and Bureau personnel had never really recovered from his one-man guerrilla assault upon the mesa which had successfully spiked their prime weapon, the explosives beneath the stockade. Immediately after that, their cannon and cannoneers along with the gunpowder, explosives and shells all went up in one almighty fireball.

The extent and framework of the Dabney-Harrelson attack plan had been made clear to Halliday the moment he located the buried leads, and Cunningham and Red Man had figured it out for themselves subsequently.

Dabney knew Cunningham was en route to the Black Hills to meet with the Sioux and trade his rifles. The plan to abandon the stockade after packing it with explosives and concealing the cannon atop the mesa and the fighters by the river to mop up the survivors following the big bang, had been Dabney's; Harrelson's rogue troopers had implemented it.

It would surely have succeeded murderously, but for one man.

Halliday was still groggy and looked like a wagon accident survivor as eager hands helped him down through the talus to the slopes. Where he was greeted by cheers from the gunrunner survivors and war whoops of approval from the Sioux.

He was the hero of the battle of Crow Creek Stockade, or at least so Caraso was proclaiming as they paused for a still half-deaf and thick-headed Halliday to grab a breather.

'Here he is, *muchachas*! You try to kill him, you lock him in chains, you chase him like a dog across the evil lands not once but two times, and still he escapes. But does he leave you all to fall victims to the very bad Bluecoats and the most evil Señor Colonel Dabney? He does not. No. When he has left you with the faces full of eggs, and is free, he returns to risk his noble life to save your miserable asses—'

'Yeah, OK, OK,' Halliday interrupted, sensing this diatribe might be rubbing some of the sheen from his moment of glory, which he knew from experience would prove all too brief in any case. 'I reckon they get the idea.' He frowned. 'Howcome you figured it was me?'

'Not guessed – knew, *compadre*,' came the exuberant reply. 'First our scouts find the dun horse up behind the granite bluffs. I say this means you were here, but nobody would believe me. But when the mesa she erupts like the end of the world, I know. I shout . . . nobody else but you would be so crazy as this—'

'Yeah, we get the general idea.' Halliday glanced around. Indians, Chinese and Americans were approaching a little apprehensively to express their gratitude. Fighting men aware of the contribution another fighting man had made to ensure their survival and ultimate victory.

He ignored them. He was wearying of the hero role already. He ducked his head instinctively as rifle fire stormed sharply upriver on the far side. But the shooting proved too distant to pose any threat. He straightened and heard a death rattle where men were attending a shot-up soldier close by. *C'est la guerre*, in spades.

Shrugging off the supporting hands, he squared his shoulders and began threading his way through the brush towards the surrey drawn up some distance away by the river bank.

Comparisons with wartime America were all too easy to make with this sobering scene. But Buck Halliday didn't have to go back that far. The dangerous way of life he still followed at times ensured that the spectacle of dead men and weeping widows was still as common as corn in Kansas. Made a man wonder if he was living right sometimes. . . .

A familiar figure rose from behind a fire to block his path. Abilene carried his left arm in a sling and displayed a gouging red bullet burn across his neck. Even so, the gunman appeared as dangerous as ever as he spoke in a voice like falling stones.

'Guess we owe it all to you, hotshot.'

'Guess you do.'

'Why'd you do it?'

'Not for you, that's for sure.'

'Cocky for a man about to die, ain't you?'

Halliday glanced around. He saw no sign of a second slim-hipped gunman with a built-in sneer.

He said, 'Where's your gun buddy?'

The gunman gestured. 'Walked into a bullet on the bluffs just as we were finishing them off.'

'Couldn't have happened to a nicer fellow.'

Abilene's face filled with fury. 'You upstart, big-headed son of a whore! You still don't get it, do you?'

Halliday felt a wave of weariness. 'Get what?'

'Sergei, is what.' Abilene dropped hand to gunbutt. 'He was my pard and you butchered him like a hog. I've been waiting my chance to square you for that. Now I got it. I always knew I had the edge on you, now you're gonna know it—'

His rage choked his words off and he was jerking sixgun from leather. Moments earlier, Halliday would not have believed he had a draw and clear left in him. But facing sudden death, he slapped iron and jerked his sixgun clear, likely as fast as he'd ever done. For a moment out of time he stared at Abilene's hate-ridden face – whose gun was still just

clearing leather. He realized in horror that he could-
n't shoot. In desperation he instead charged the
man, slamming his left hand down on the leaping .45
then crashing his own weapon against the hardcase's
head with all his power.

Abilene went down as though his legs had been
sliced from beneath him. Halliday sucked his jarred
knuckles and spat blood.

It hit him then. He'd risked death rather than
shoot. He held the Colt up and stared at it dumbly. It
looked different and felt alien in his fist. It was as
though the slaughter of the past hour had proven
too much even for action-hungry Buck Halliday.

He couldn't shoot Abilene, even though the man
was hell bent on killing him.

That was something to ponder on if ever he had a
quiet moment.

It had grown quiet about him and men were staring at this big dark figure bathed in fire glow, then at
the unconscious man at his feet. Halliday raised his
chin and sensed that that which he had expected to
pass, was already passing. The brushfire of violence
had raged and been quenched. Maybe it would stay
that way. Who could tell?

Gradually all the harshness went from his face as,
passing through a knot of riflemen leaning on their
weapons, he came face to face with Lu Nin and was
relieved to see her safe and well.

'Hi, lovely lady.' He felt light-headed. He didn't
realize he was swaying slightly. 'Guess we made it. . . .'

'You are a mess,' she said calmly, standing on tip-
toes to swab grime off his face with a wet cloth. Then

she smiled and whispered: 'I knew I would see you again.'

And Halliday smiled, maybe his first genuine smile in too long. Lu Nin returned his smile as he glanced towards the hunched figure of Cunningham seated in his surrey nearby. The man was speaking with a grinning Caraso and a Chinese, when the sudden chatter of gunfire mingled with thudding hoofbeats sounded upriver and close.

Hands snatched up weapons as riders erupted from willows and conifers to lift their mounts, then to leap from the western bluffs to crash into the river. There followed giant bursts of spray. They were hotly pursued from the timber by feathered riders holding flaring guns.

'By God, it's Dabney!'

It was Cunningham who shouted as Halliday was already legging it along the bank, grim-faced and empty-handed.

Dabney was struck down when almost to the near bank. As he swayed in his saddle, his escorts surged past him, faces pale, hard and grim in the flickering light as they cut loose at the nearest enemy target, the big, wide-shouldered figure in black-grimed rig.

Halliday dived full length as the taller man shouted. 'It's Halliday, the dirty turncoat bastard!' His companion screamed something unintelligible and both were blasting as they spurred up the bank away from the lurching figure of Dabney, horses streaming water, gunsmoke fogging thick and white.

But their target was belly-flat, while the murderous crash of Caraso's double-barrelled shotgun shouted a song of death in the wild night.

The shorter rider went first, throwing up both arms in a paroxysm of agony to go plunging beneath the surface, waters turning crimson as the body bobbed away.

The surviving half of the Neat Twins, Cole, made it halfway up the bank slope before man and horse were smashed backwards before a leaden scythe.

Bullets chopped the water around the tilting figure of Dabney, but Halliday's shout rose above the noise. 'He's done for. A man with half an eye could see that.'

The guns fell silent and Dabney slumped upon his horse's streaming neck.

'Why, Buck?' he croaked. 'You were with me . . . with me. . . . You owed me!'

Halliday, towering against a backdrop of moon-wash, smoke and fire glow, glanced downstream to pick out a slender silhouette by Dabney's surrey.

'Things change,' he said.

'Water,' croaked the dying man, but when one of the Chinese made to respond, Cunningham spoke sharply from his surrey.

'No! No water. No anything.'

Dabney looked up haggardly from his bloody pallet on the grass which was encircled by fighters, most of whom were getting their first look at the man who had been backing both the miners and the troopers in their battles with the Sioux and the gunrunners.

The first look and the last.

Dabney knew he was dying, and was afraid. All his life he'd been prone to attacks of terror and failure of the spirit. He had lied, deceived, slandered, persecuted and even killed to conceal his weakness from the world. But now it was clear for all to see here along the banks of the Singing River tonight. The colonel was terrified of death and wept in his terror.

'Water! Buck – won't you?'

Halliday picked up a ladle and leaned towards the water bucket, but Cunningham's emotional cry halted him.

'No, man, no! He can have all the water he wants, all the help we can give him, but only when he confesses.' He leaned from his rig and thrust an accusing finger at the man on the pallet. 'You ruined my name, my career, my health and my life, Colonel. Confess it now or go thirsty into hell – and damn your evil soul!'

Staring at the cripple, Halliday sensed for the first time perhaps that he was genuine in his outrage and sense of persecution, having imagined before that it might have been just a smokescreen to cover the simple fact that he was just a bitter loser.

'Yes!' gasped Dabney. 'All right, whatever you say, Major. I turned back from helping you that day at Vicksburg as I could see the enemy was about to overrun your position, and there was nothing my company could do to save you. I admit it, now—'

'And the court martial when I survived with a broken back and was accused of cowardice,' Cunningham shouted. 'You testified that I'd ordered retreat, which provided you with the reason you needed to explain your failure to follow orders. But you lied before the court, didn't you? You placed your hand on the Bible and flag and swore I had shown cowardice – and damned me in the eyes of my country.'

A long moment passed before Dabney nodded weakly.

'Yes, I lied. Everything you say is true. Now can I—'

'Do you hear that?' Cunningham shouted wildly, his excitement extraordinary to witness. 'Ten years, but cleared at last.'

And all saw the changes taking place before their eyes, the deep and bitter lines leeching from the man's face, some hint of the boyishness returning as friend, enemy, the indifferent and the involved, all came to realize just how huge the burden this man had been carrying so long, yet less the burden of the mangled body but rather that of the spirit.

Dabney had killed Major Cunningham at Vicksburg but had brought him back to life at Singing River.

It affected everybody to see it. But a sober Halliday sensed it might be affecting Cunningham's wife more than anyone.

The morning wind blowing across the sprawling badlands stirred Lu Nin's glossy tresses as she stood, slender and composed, facing the east.

Halliday stood at the woman's side with the dun's lines looped over his shoulder. In back of the couple were the lame, the halt, the wounded and the haggard survivors of yet another bloody clash in the

Black Hills. He suspected the incident like so many others would mean little in the annals of the West. He had no way of suspecting that each mine sunk here, each shot fired and each drop of blood shed would in time lead as inexorably as destiny to some future day on Little Big Horn River when the Sioux would rise up and strike back in a way America would never forget.

They'd cut back out of the hills overnight after the scouts reported the massing of miners making for the stockade to support what was left of the late Captain Harrelson's troops.

Cunningham was returning to his remote sanctuary to help them to fight. He insisted he'd sold his last gun, that the need was now gone – and Halliday believed him.

As did his wife.

'He needs me now,' Lu Nin said softly. 'I wanted only to escape before, but now he has found his pride again it would be too cruel for me to leave.'

'Sure, I understand.'

A telling moment. Their lives had touched dramatically and maybe something strong and true had sprung up between them. Halliday knew he must let her go but seemed reluctant to do so, something accurately observed by just one other sharp-eyed survivor of the holocaust.

Teo Caraso approached from the remuda, big hat hanging down his dusty back by the throat strap, rowel spurs jingling musically in sharp contrast to the Mexican's unusually serious mood. For what he'd just heard Halliday say, and what his instincts were telling him, told him he should speak up now instead of keeping his surprise until they dusted up to the title gate of the Circle H.

'*Señor amigo. . . ?*'

'Beat it.' Halliday was looking at Lu Nin, wanting to go, needing to stay.

'The horses.'

Halliday turned in irritation. 'What freakin' horses? If you're goin' to start in tellin' me how your damned mule and that moron Devil—'

'No, the horses back home. You said you would shoot me if just one of our fine animals was gone or dead when we get home, because I leave them to come save you . . .'

'I will. You can believe it.'

'Ah, so ungrateful, just like always—'

'Will you get to hell while I finish what I'm sayin' to the lady!'

Caraso's skinny chest swelled. 'Your horses are being tended, *compañero*. She is there.'

'She who?'

'Señorita Cable. Your sweetheart.'

Halliday paled. He shot a glance at Lu Nin, who appeared to be smiling. Then he seized Caraso by the shirt and shook him roughly.

'Idiot! It's all over with us. We broke up. Why do you reckon I went to Paradise to get drunk that day?'

The Mexican broke loose and massaged his neck.

'I ask Missy to keep the eye on the horses and she say she would move into the house until we get back. She say not to tell you this . . . because she is as stubborn and proud as you.' He spread both hands wide.

'But she still loves you. She tells this to Caraso. She also say you would grow up some day and if she had not found some rich ranchero to wed, she would still be waiting when that day comes.'

Halliday stared. The man was speaking the truth. He could tell. He wheeled sharply. Lu Nin was gone.

After what seemed a long time – it was actually the most telling minute in Halliday's life – he nodded and said quietly. 'Well, in that case, we'd best be headin' home, then.'

He didn't realize he was smiling in a way he'd never done before as the horses carried them away, and the wind blew softly from the south.